Simon & the Oaks

'An enthralling saga set in Sweden about the lives of two boys before, during and after the Second World War . . . It's impossible to put down' *The Times*

'Absorbing and tautly constructed . . . Fredriksson is gifted with both the insights of maturity and the art of the storyteller' *Jewish Chronicle*

'A wondrous and winding story . . . the thrilling descriptions of countryside and nature are fascinating' *Berliner Morgenpost*

'Grips the reader from the first page to the last . . . this novel is imbued with brightness from the shimmering light of the sea' *Sudkurier*

Hanna's Daughters

'Gripping and gritty . . . Catherine Cookson with a touch of Strindberg' Marika Cobbold

'Extremely moving . . . hypnotically readable' *Spectator*

'Hanna and her daughters are hard to shake off, lingering long after you've turned the last page . . . Profound, moving . . . rich in detail' *She*

'The writing is exquisite . . . For me, finding this gem of an author was a true and marvellous discovery' *Toronto Record*

'Grips you from the first page to the last. Marianne Fredriksson succeeds, apparently effortlessly, in portraying rural life at the end of the 19th century ... The reader follows almost breathlessly the lives of the three women, and the compelling, moving descriptions of their destinies' *Oldenburgische Volkszeitung (Book of the Week)*

'A wonderful book. The family chronicle, a kind of story which once produced the greatest novels, now seems to be experiencing a renaissance' *Die Welt*

Also by Marianne Fredriksson
HANNA'S DAUGHTERS
SIMON & THE OAKS

Inge & Mira

Marianne Fredriksson

Translated by Anna Paterson

ORION

Original title: *Flyttfaglar*
Published by Wahlstrom & Widstrand, Stockholm, 1999

Published by agreement with Bengt Nordin Agency,
Varmdo, Sweden

This edition first published in Great Britain in 2000 by
Orion
An imprint of Orion Books Ltd
Orion House, 5 Upper St Martin's Lane,
London WC2H 9EA

A CIP catalogue record for this book is available
from the British Library

Typeset in Great Britain by
Deltatype Ltd, Birkenhead, Merseyside

Printed and bound by
Clays Ltd, St Ives plc

ACKNOWLEDGEMENTS

A heartfelt thank you to Luisa, who generously let me share not only her recollections of her native Chile and her memories of its colours and scents, but also her thoughtful reflections about Sweden where she has created a new life for herself and her children.

But it is not her life that is described in this book. I have used my imagination to write a novel about a handful of immigrants into an alien country with its own customs and prejudices.

FOREWORD

This is a story about two women who became friends.

The way they had led their lives could hardly have been more different.

Each had been allotted her own climate: long dark winter nights to one, days of burning sunshine to the other. One woman was a sceptic who put her trust in reason; and the other talked intimately with God every day.

But, in fact, they had things in common: both were divorced and both had to cope with the children on their own – and although these children were now adults, both mothers were eaten up with pointless worry over them.

The two women were the same age, almost fifty, and had started keeping count of their winkles. They had realised that they were on a kind of slippery slope. Aware that they must die one day. And that it meant that they had to be prepared to forgive themselves.

The winter-woman wrote a diary. At times she believed it allowed her to speak openly in a way she had not dared before. But that was not true: she had always been frank.

Maybe she was looking for a pattern.

On the first blank page she had written: 'Why do I feel this need to create a reflected image of such an unremarkable life? Is it because I am searching for what might lie behind the mirror?' She rarely found any answers but carried on filling up page after page; she wrote about little everyday things and about the great questions of being.

This was what she wrote on 28 March 1988: 'It's raining today, the snow is retreating on all fronts. Am I imagining it or does the black earth smell of spring?'

The same day she wrote at the bottom of the page: 'When one is hurt, what feels the pain?'

The other one, the sun-woman, did not keep a diary, even though she spoke two languages: she thought in Spanish and cursed in Swedish. She felt no need to reflect on hurt and pain, because she understood them already. And she was as furious with the pain each time she felt it.

Some of those who died, and were lost to her, were irreplaceable. She had pushed them away, out of her life. Or, at least, they had no business being here in her new country. She was uncertain about Sweden. She was uncertain about her native country too: she hated it but longed to be back.

The great verities did not concern her. Her whole life had been taken up by the need to survive.

Her most striking feature was the look of intent in her eyes; her appetite for life was a source of joy.

And yet she knew better than most that behind both joy and terror stood death. And that this was why all choices were important.

Every night she had a conversation with God.

Even so, she was not sure that she believed in Him.

CHAPTER I

We met in the garden centre.

We were separated by a huge trolley, some three metres by eight, filled with thousands of pansies. An unruly blue and purple sea, with flashes of yellow like waves glittering in the sun.

She was standing directly opposite me, and her face reflected my own delight. I gestured towards the flowers, saying something about how wonderful they looked. She smiled broadly and replied that there was nothing like flowers for making you feel that life's worth living. 'Or maybe small children too,' she added. This startled me. She spoke good but accented Swedish and I realised she must be an immigrant, perhaps from Chile.

'I haven't thought about it like that,' I said. 'But you're right, of course.'

Then we both reacted to the wind rattling the panes in the roof of the tall greenhouse and agreed that it was too early in the year to plant out pansies. Every night still brought a touch of frost. 'And then there's the wind,' she said.

We hugged our coats tighter as we walked from the greenhouse to the shop.

'My name's Ingegerd,' I told her. 'People call me Inge.'

'And I'm called Edermira, but here in Sweden it's Mira.'

We nodded, as if to signify that things somehow felt right. I was curious about her.

A little later Mira was speaking quickly and eagerly to the girl behind the counter. She was asking for the bulbs of . . . She was forced to halt, closed her eyes, thought and found the right name. In Spanish.

The shop assistant twisted the corners of her mouth into a smile that was both anxious and scornful. Then she laughed, shrugged and said, turning to me, 'Do you know what she's on about?'

I answered awkwardly, blushing with shame: 'She's asking for African blue lilies.'

I tried to catch Mira's eyes and said, 'They stick to tulips in this place. Let's go.'

But my voice faltered when I registered how furious she was. it was a deep black fury shot through with red, and crackling like electricity. Her entire being seemed to spark. For the first time I realised her inner force.

We left, to trudge along in a wind that pierced coats and sweaters.

I was freezing.

Mira seemed unaware of the cold.

Down by the water's edge the sun slipped through the grey. We found shelter behind a rock and turned our faces up towards the light. There was so much I wanted to tell her: how ashamed I was and how it was true that every natioin had its share of stupid people. That the girl in the garden centre was just being silly, not nasty. And probably anxious, I also wanted to say.

But I stayed silent, because these were the kind of words that fall flat, the kind that leave no trace, let alone grow any roots. A kind of hopelessness was gnawing at my insides; nothing could put this right.

On an impulse I put my arm round Mira's shoulder, but realised at once that I was overstepping the mark. I withdrew and instead pointed at the sky: 'See those gulls? They're heading for my lawn to hunt for worms.'

Mira was not interested. She said, 'I'm always so conscious of my dignity.'

Overhead, the gulls are now screeching so loudly I had to shout to make myself heard: 'I'm just the same. I think it's to do with getting older.'

I fell silent for bit, ashamed again, then added: 'But, of course, it's different . . .'

'Yes, that's right. I'm sure you're respected wherever you go.'

The sun succeeded against all odds and broke through. The sky has a purple tinge.

The sea turned blue.

We looked at each other smiling. I noted that the sheen had returned to her honey-coloured skin. Her hair seemed to have settled back into place; she wore it in a smart short cut.

'I went to Madeira last autumn,' I told her. 'In November, when the weather here is at its worst. There were rootstocks of *Agapanthus africanus* for sale in Funchal market and I bought about a dozen. I've potted them up and keep them in my greenhouse. At least three are in leaf. Why don't you come home with me and I'll give you some?'

Then I felt uneasy: maybe this, too, was intrusive. 'I've only got a small modern terraced house, you see, and the garden is small too. There's no room for ten new pots. Besides, these Afros grow into big bushy things.'

And we laughed together, at last.

We got up and walked along the beach. She moved quickly, with long purposeful strides.

I followed her, calling: 'Slow down!'

3

She stopped and waited for me, with a small apologetic grin.

'Gosh, you're fit,' I said.

Later I saw that those big strides were second nature to her. She leapt along as if over hurdles, up steps, across floors and lawns.

'I'm always in a hurry,' she said.

Then the path along the beach came to an end and the suburban streets began. I stopped and said as I looked out over the water, 'I was born near the sea. It pulls at me – sometimes it even seems to be part of me. I feel a kind of affinity with it.'

I was embarrassed but she listened seriously, nodding as if she understood: 'I, too, grew up near water. It was a river. I would slip off down to the bank when I was little. Though we were not allowed to.'

Her eyes looked far away, lost in memory: they were not as brown as I had thought, they had green lights.

'I loved thinking about the Rio Mapocho, how it tumbled from the snowy peaks of the Andes, rushed down the mountains, picking up speed and power on the slopes. How, up there in the mountains, the river flowed with pure clear water.'

She was quiet for a while, her face seemed to tighten.

'But then the Rio Mapocho has to run through Santiago and picks up so much filth. When it reached the suburb where I lived, it was brown and sluggish.'

I nodded, and said that my sea was dirty too, that the entire Baltic Sea was polluted; the bottom was lifeless.

'Oh, how awful,' she said, but her voice sounded sour. I said nothing.

We were both still silent as we walked the last stretch to my house. She was trying to adjust her speed to mine.

4

Suddenly she said, 'I'm sure you must have seen my river on TV. Pinochet's soldiers threw corpses into the Mapocho.'

I did not dare tell her the truth: that I closed my eyes when the images on the screen became unbearable.

CHAPTER 2

I was proud of my greenhouse. It wasn't grand, or especially pretty, but the panes were made of armoured glass, there were heating-coils under the floor and ventilation panels in the roof that opened automatically when it got too hot. My large potted plants were kept there during the cold half of the year, the orange trees with their yellow fruits, the lemon trees with their seemingly permanent clusters of scented flowers.

At this time of the year, in early spring, the greenhouse served as a nursery garden. The annuals had started to sprout in the peat pots that covered benches and shelving; in June, once the risk of night frosts was past, the seedlings were put outside.

A nasturtium, ready to burst out of its pot, had plenty of large flame-coloured buds. 'This is nice,' Mira said. She sounded happy.

I told her that this was my way of coping with the interminable wait for spring.

Mira talked about her south-west-facing balcony. It was glazed, and there was a long bench. Her idea was to place the African lilies at each end of the bench and to line up pink geraniums between them.

Mira loved symmetry.

Together we studied my geraniums from last year. They looked dead.

'I'll deal with them this weekend, one way or the other,' I said. 'Cut them right back and replant in bigger pots.'

'They're not still alive, are they?' Mira sounded surprised.

'They are,' I said, and launched into an explanation – in my lecturing voice, which I detested.

I fell silent and instead found the plants I had bought in Madeira. We both noticed right away that the roots were about to break through the peat pots.

'They've come on – that's good!' Mira said, jubilant. I replied that it was time I got large terracotta pots and new potting compost.

We arranged that she would come back in a week or so to see how they were getting on in their new setting.

'Would you like a cup of coffee?'

'Yes, please.'

We went into the kitchen. I filled the kettle. 'Only instant, I'm afraid.'

'Is there any tea?'

I rummaged in the grocery cupboard and found a packet. Good. Also some American cookies, rather old, but still . . .

'And do you live here alone?'

She sounded so formal. Somehow, I had to make her feel more relaxed, but could not think how.

'Yes, I'm divorced.'

'Me too.'

Our eyes met. Before long we were talking about our children. As women do.

'I've got two daughters. They're grown-up now.'

'I have two sons,' she said, and I could hear the pride in

her voice. Her face lit up, then saddened. 'They've become so Swedish.'

'You must be pleased, surely?'

I could hear myself again: it sounded wrong.

'Yes, I suppose so,' she said. 'Sometimes I worry about it. Especially when they trust people. That's so Swedish. Chileans should not be naïve, they should know better.'

'Are you saying that the Swedes cheat your sons?'

Now she is embarrassed, but she does not give up. 'No one has done that. Not yet.' I did not dare laugh, but she did. 'I'm so silly sometimes.'

I kept quiet but reflected that mothers always find reason to worry.

Suddenly she said, 'I used to think I had been born again when I came to Sweden because here I was valued as a human being.' Her smile was apologetic, as if to excuse the solemnity of her words. 'But can a thirty-year-old who's had children speak of being born?'

'Tell me what happened.'

'We crossed the straits from Kastrup and got to the railway station in Malmö. Even though it was nine o'clock in the morning, it was so dark. It looked strange. Suddenly we heard music and saw people in a procession, carrying a statue of a saint. I thought, They're Christian after all. When they got closer I realised the "saint" was actually walking and that there were electric candles in her hair. Even so, the strangest thing of all was that she was singing, loudly but tonelessly, although the musicians following her were playing the right notes. She was quite fat, too. I decided that in this country the saints are ordinary people. I think that's marvellous.'

'Go on,' I said, once we had stopped giggling.

'Then the train got going, gathered speed, *dunk-dunk,*

fast, faster. Dawn came slowly, time dragged, but I thought that sooner or later it would make up its mind. Then it was light, and I saw forest for the first time in my life. It had been snowing and the trees were bending under the layers of white. It was so very white!' Mira's face expressed the astonishment she had felt.

'From our window at home, I could see the snow covering the tops of the Andes, and I used to fantasize about what it was like up there. About a white world, turning blue in the twilight. So far away, impossible to reach.'

Her gaze lost itself in the distance.

'My mother always said, "It's just frozen rain." But Father told me that Chile's wild Indians lived there, famous warrior tribes who had fought and won in battles against the Incas and the Spaniards.'

I poured more tea, lit the candles on the kitchen table and planned to tell her that I'd like to know more about these Indian tribes.

But Mira wanted to follow her own train of thought. She remembered in images, as if there was a camera in her brain, and developing apparatus, which must not be disturbed when it was in motion.

'We stopped at a station somewhere and nothing could've stopped my boys from dashing outside. They went crazy, kicked the white stuff, squeezed it in their hands, licked it and shouted, "Nana, it's like a soft ice-cream!" When they came back inside they were cold and wet.

'And then the train passed through forest again, but after a few hours and landscape opened up. We passed beautiful red-painted houses, with huge barns. Those must be country estates, we thought. When the train rolled into towns and villages, we saw family homes. And taller houses with large windows, and balconies with fir trees on them. It was just before Christmas.

'I remember thinking, where do ordinary people live? Ordinary poor people.' She laughed, and was still smiling as she continued her story. 'Then an amazing thing happened. The guard came into our carriage and said something about a Chilean being on the train. He tried using sign language, but we didn't really understand – except that he meant well. Then another man came in and greeted us in Spanish. He said his name was Luís, and that he had been born in Valparaiso. We were no longer alone among strangers. He said that many Chileans were living in Sweden, and that he had been in the country for over ten years. He was a Swedish citizen now. You could hear the pride in his voice.

'We were a big group, eighteen, and the men asked him many questions. He seemed to have all the answers. He talked about politics and how there was democracy, and about the Immigration Bureau and immigration permits. I didn't understand much of all that.

' "The Swedes are well informed about Chile. They know about the military coup, the torture and the disappearances. They read about it in their newspapers and watch the hell-hole that is Chile on TV," Luís said.

'I felt ashamed. I knew nothing about Sweden – had never even heard of it before I arrived here. But Luís went on to say that Sweden was a good country and had already carried out many of the reforms Allende had dreamed of for Chile.

'Next, he told us – and now I was *really* listening – that in Sweden men and women had equal rights. "Women earn their own money and make their own decisions. There are women in government positions here," he said, and laughed at our surprise. He also said that Latin-American

9

men were often in trouble with the Swedish police. For one thing, the law forbids men to hit women.

' "But what if she has been cheating on him with another man?" a young man asked; he had been recently married.

' "It's her right to be unfaithful. She is responsible for her own life and her own body," Luís answered.

' "That's madness!" cried the man, and many agreed angrily.

' "But consider this," Luís said. "In Chile adulterous men aren't punished. And, remember, I told you that women and men have equal rights here."

'After this, you could hear women laughing through the men's shouts. I was so surprised that I sat there with my mouth open. I was speechless. I glanced at my husband, but his face was blank. Then I, too, laughed with the other women.

'I wanted to ask questions but did not dare. None of the women did, but their laughter sounded wild.

'Later on Luís went back to his seat in another carriage. He said goodbye to us and wished us luck. The little children were already asleep in their mother's laps, but my boys were sitting bolt upright. They looked as if they had been hypnotised by everything Luís had told us. The older one, José, put his arm round me and said, "Listen, Nana, we'll manage."

'We were served tea and sandwiches. Then the guard brought us blankets and pillows and we bedded down on the seats as best we could. It was crowded, we were jammed in together. We were tired. But before I fell asleep I was thinking that there must be a connection between what Luís had said about women in Sweden and that saint, singing in Malmö station. But I had no idea what it might be.'

★

Outside the windows of my little terraced house the twilight was gathering slowly. The long blue evening hours in March were filled with melancholy. We made more tea and drank it. Then Mira rose, saying she wanted to leave now because she disliked the dark.

We exchanged telephone numbers. I went with her to the front door. The wind had died down, and it was crisp and cold outside. 'There's another frost coming,' Mira said.

She strode away and disappeared down the road. I was left behind in the hall wondering about her.

CHAPTER 3

Mira was upset.

Why had she talked so much? She had spent years practising talking without actually saying anything, as Swedes did. Keeping a distance, agreeing, going on about weather or fashion, complaining about dark skies or the eternal snow-clearing. And gossip, of course, not about the neighbours but about celebrities whose pictures turned up in magazines. Mira could not afford to buy magazines, so she usually found herself with nothing to say – not that it mattered: she had learnt how to look interested.

During her first years in Sweden she had pondered on the native way of speaking. The point must be to avoid close contact with others, she decided.

Which seemed a good idea to her, at least in the beginning.

For a time she took great pains to be like the Swedes, to assimilate. Eventually she realised that this was impossible;

the colour of her skin marked her out as different. And the way she spoke. And her background, her experiences of a world with different attitudes and manners.

Swedes liked people who stood out from the crowd. But only if they fitted in. Bloody hell, she thought, in Swedish. She did not dare use Spanish for curses.

What was so special about the woman who had made her speak openly? Inge Bertilsson had been interested, curious and, frighteningly, empathetic. But she did not truly understand. And that was why Mira had told her about the dead bodies in the river.

Fucking stupid, she thought, in their language again.

By the time she was unlocking her own front door, she felt ashamed. She remembered how she had tried to talk to Inge formally, in order to establish the difference between them. She did not usually behave like that, but she had sensed some kind of barrier and it had to do with social class.

Class difference was one of the things the Swedes simply refused to admit existed. This annoyed Mira.

She had spotted it the moment she was led through the rooms in Inge's house; rooms, which boasted somehow of their simplicity. Upper-class homes were often like that here. Pine flooring, rugs, bookshelves everywhere, all filled to bursting, the overflow ending up on chairs and tables. Odd-looking pictures on the walls, armchairs like hammocks with seats made from plaited canvas straps rather than proper upholstery. And often dusty and untidy.

Mira herself had chosen soft leather-covered armchairs and a flower-patterned carpet. And her house was tidy.

Inge was one of those decent Swedes, whose unchanging friendliness made you wonder what they were really thinking.

She watched the evening news on TV: a high-pressure area was approaching. The sun would shine and the risk of night frosts increase.

Later, when she was getting ready for bed, she felt sad rather than angry. As she washed, brushed her teeth and put on her nightdress, she thought of Inge, how open she was.

And Mira realised she herself must have needed to talk.

In bed, she talked to God, as she always did. He agreed that Mira had been withdrawn.

She fell asleep and the dreams came, a rush of images from childhood. They never stayed with her in the morning when she woke, but the sensation of light and intimacy remained after the night-time mirages had faded.

She made some coffee, sat at the kitchen table for a while and concentrated on remembering, which she had not done for ages.

She was seven years old and had just crawled through the hole in the wall, then flitted along the lanes, straight ahead at first then left, down to the river. That was not allowed, which made it extra exciting.

Then she heard the rumbling noise of the river and soon she could see it, follow the flow of the current with her eyes. This was when she tried to imagine how the river began, far away in the high Andes. She also thought about its purpose. Where was it going?

Her father had said it wanted to reach the sea, the greatest ocean in the world.

Why did the river long for the ocean, which would just swallow it up?

The Pacific Ocean. She liked thinking about that name. Once she had been allowed to go with her father to see it, when he still had the lorry. She had seen it then, the great endless sea. It was not at peace, not in the slightest. It roared, and its vast waves beat against the rocks.

The most extraordinary thing was that they could travel up the rock-faces in lifts. There were seventeen – she knew because she had counted them.

Here, on the banks of the river Mapocho, tired, filthy men dug up the riverside clay, poured water over it and stirred it to a sticky consistency then mixed it with straw. Next they put it into square wooden moulds to shape it and left the clay bricks to dry in the sun. This was the building material for the houses along the lanes and all the garden walls in this suburb.

The brown slimy clay smelt terrible. Dead cats and dogs came floating down the river and ended up on the banks. That was exciting.

Then the little girl looked up at the sun and realised that hours had passed. She did not dare go home, not before her father got back from work. He defended her if mother was cross. And she would be cross.

She crept back along the lane, keeping to the wall in the deep shadow thrown by the low sun, then into Graciela's house. As usual at this time of day it was full of women. They were chatting and hardly noticed her.

The voices rose and fell, and sometimes they shouted to each other. Now and then they laughed together at some story full of bad words. The child understood what the words meant but never grasped the jokes.

The women complained most of the time, and cursed, and sometimes wept bitterly. The little girl thought there was more than one woman in each of them – angry women and sad ones.

Sometimes one of them screamed so loudly that the little girl's mother, sitting at her sewing machine, could hear her through the walls. She would say that the devil had taken the screaming woman.

This was exciting. Every time the little girl hid in the corner of Graciela's house, she longed to see the devil take one of the women.

She herself had been told there was a devil inside her. It had frightened her at first, until she realised it was an Indian. It scared people.

When she was teased at school, she would hit out and shout that they should keep away from her, her grandfather was a real *mapocho* warrior. Wild Indian blood ran in Mira's veins.

They left her alone after that.

It was a useful devil. Later on she learnt at school that everyone on Earth is pursued by seven demons, all dangerous. Only when you have stood up fearlessly to the demons will your guardian angel appear. The priest had told them this. And Mira, who had faced only one of her demons, believed she would never meet her angel.

And that was true enough, she thought, and poured more coffee. And returned to Graciela's house.

The women were scattering now because the men were on their way home from work and each woman had to hurry off to call her children then cook a meal.

The little girl had decided that the men were easier to understand and safer too. They had their devils, of course, but these seemed more straightforward. The men's devils were in bottles and only escaped when too much red wine flowed. But it grew dangerous when the bottles contained *aguardiente*, a spirit coloured red with plum juice. Unlike the women, the little girl was unafraid because she could rely on her swift feet.

Mira was washing up in her nice Swedish kitchen when

she made up her mind. She would phone Inge. Not to apologise, but to offer help with the potting-up.

CHAPTER 4

Inge Bertilsson no longer worked as a teacher and lived instead on her income from writing books, often about children and their schooling. This suited her well, because she had university degrees in education and Swedish literature. But her chief resource was the years she had spent in the real world.

She enjoyed her work, but it was lonely sometimes, especially now, when both her daughters were in England to study the language.

She might have befriended the unpredictable Latin woman simply for company, as a change from her usual solitude. But no – there was more to it: there was an attraction, a spark, perhaps, between them. She searched for the right word, gave up and cursed her constant need for definitions.

When the phone rang, she hoped for a moment that it might be one of her girls. But no, she mustn't be silly: they had no money to waste on international calls. It had to be her publishers.

When she heard that deep, accented voice, she was surprised: she felt elated.

Mira said she wanted to help. Maybe with potting-up. The geraniums as well as the African lilies. It would be heavy work, dragging soil and potting compost around the place. Then her confidence wavered: 'But only if it suits you,' she said.

'Of course it does,' Inge answered, cheerfully.

They arranged to meet. Inge would be waiting in her car outside Mira's front door at ten o'clock next Saturday morning. Did she know how to find her way? Yes, no problem.

'There's a garden centre in Eskilsta. It's not bad. And it's cheap. Let's go there.'

Mira laughed. She understood. That old nursery garden – never again.

''Bye, see you,' they said to each other. Inge stayed by the telephone and looked at it gratefully: Mira had sounded relaxed and informal.

Still, when they met next Saturday morning they were both awkward and shy. Inge mentioned the weather, the blessed sunshine. Mira agreed.

Somehow they needed time to calm down. But after a while Inge said: 'I have been thinking about that story of your arrival in Sweden. You told it beautifully . . . but, well, I got the impression you weren't really *there* . . . that you felt detached from it.'

The question hung in the air. Mira was grateful not to have to make eye-contact with Inge, whose gaze was fixed on the road ahead. Inge continued, 'I thought that maybe you've told it so many times it's become like a film that's shown again and again?'

Dear Lord, please, Mira thought, please let us get there soon.

Her prayer was answered. Inge turned the car down the slip-road into the big garden centre. The car park was crowded so it took a little time to find a space.

But when they were getting out of the car, Mira

remembered that God had agreed that she could be stuck up. So she said, 'You see, I have to force myself not to remember things.'

'While you were travelling?'

'Yes, and later on as well. The memories don't belong in Sweden. Can you understand that?'

'I'm trying to.'

Inge was about to say that this was surely like leading a double life. Instead she stayed silent; she felt ashamed because once more she had got too close.

They were looking at a mountainous pile of potting compost, wrapped in heavy plastic, white and neat.

'I usually pick the ten-kilogram bags. I can't lift the big ones.'

'No problem.' Mira had soon shifted three twenty-kilogram sacks into the wheelbarrow.

'Gosh, you're something else,' Inge said.

The pots were easier, fifteen medium-sized ones for the geraniums and ten big ones for the Afros. They went into the barrow and then to the boot of the car.

As usual when she met someone practical, Inge felt inadequate. Weakly, she crept over to the till and paid.

'How much was it?'

'Not a lot. Couple of hundred.'

'I'll pay my share.'

The Swedish woman did not speak. Mira noticed that her companion was red-faced and that she sounded angry when she said, 'Don't even think about it.'

They did not speak as the car followed the twisting roads towards Inge's house. Both of them knew something crucial had been said, but neither could work out what it was. In the end Inge said, 'I had hoped that we would become friends. A friend is someone who can accept a well-meant gift.'

Mira forced herself to say, 'There's something you should know. I always get angry with my friends.'

'I won't forget,' Inge said, laughing.

She's all right, Mira thought. But the muscles in her face tightened, and Inge said, 'Why are you angry?'

But Mira was not angry. She was afraid.

'We must wear wellingtons. You can borrow a pair of mine, but they're probably too big for you. Maybe with a pair of thick socks.'

'But I've got large feet, that's why I run along so fast.'

They were chatting easily, and as brightly as the dazzling sunshine that filled the greenhouse. Mira fetched the compost bags and the pots. Inge put the new pots into a large basin of water. They had to soak for an hour.

'Come on, let's have some soup in the meantime,' Inge said.

CHAPTER 5

She had cheese and fresh bread, but just one bag of dried vegetable soup.

'It's not bad,' she said, as she peered short-sightedly at the instructions on the back of the bag.

'Let me help,' Mira said.

'If you like.'

Mira found a packet of corn in the freezer, a little chilli sauce left in the bottom of an old bottle, some coriander and a piece of smoked bacon. She cubed the meat and added it to the soup. Then she tasted it and added salt and pepper. 'I wish we had some parsley,' she said.

'We do. I've got a potful just outside the kitchen door.'

After a while Mira called, 'Look, you've got some thyme here. All right if I take some?'

'Of course it is.'

When they were sitting at the table eating the soup, which was very good, Inge said, 'This reminds me of an old fairy-tale about a man who could make soup by boiling a nail.'

Mira laughed. 'Not a nail,' she replied. 'This time a bag.'

They were still laughing when they returned to the greenhouse and started dealing with the pots. A layer of broken crocks on the bottom, then compost, then the plants. The geraniums sulked and looked miserable, in spite of all the care. But the Afros were responding, or at least Mira thought so.

'They've been given hope for the future,' she said.

They were up to their ankles in muddy water, with muck all over their hands and faces, when something blocked the sunlight. It was no cloud that threw a shadow over the entrance to the greenhouse, but a big man, tall and wide. He laughed and said, 'Both ladies hard at work, it seems. Can I help?'

'Oh, Nesto, you trouble-maker, I should've guessed,' Mira said, so lovingly that Inge realised immediately that the giant in the doorway was tiny Mira's son. The two spoke eagerly in fast-flowing Spanish.

'I'll go in and heat the soup again,' Inge said, when the Spanish slowed down.

'Please don't go to any trouble for me, I'm not hungry.'

'Oh, yes, you are,' Mira said. 'You're always hungry.'

Inge stopped in the doorway, trying to wipe the soil off her face, but only making it worse. She was tall, even for a Swedish woman, but he was almost a head taller. Mmm, he's attractive, she thought. Aloud, she said, 'You look just like the Red Indians I adored when I was little.'

'What? Did you know Indians?'

'Only in books. With terrific illustrations.'

'But I'm a *mestizo* – most Chileans are. Ask mother!'

His laughter made the greenhouse panes shake. Pretending to be cross, Mira told him, 'You can tidy in here while we clean ourselves up.'

'*Si, si, nana.*'

On their way to the kitchen they heard him turn on the water and start to hose down the floor. Inge called out, 'No water in the freshly planted pots, please!'

And Mira said, 'I asked to him to come round and help get the lilies back to my flat.'

'But they must stay here for a week after replanting. You know, to settle down. You'll have to come back next weekend.'

Mira nodded and a big smile spread over her face. Her teeth looked whiter than ever against her dirty skin.

'Your son is incredibly charming,' Inge said.

'I know. It's his big problem.'

'I almost see what you mean,' Inge answered, and in that instant, she remembered him, the boy in the first row at the desk next to the door. The image became sharper as she washed and changed into clean clothes and shoes. In that class of immigrant children, he had been by far the brightest. He was eager and inventive, understood and learnt quickly. Happy about himself, full of questions and new ideas. But idle, never did his homework, never learnt to spell in Swedish.

When they had sat down at the table to have the soup, with the cheese, the warm bread and a bottle of red wine from Chile, Inge said, 'I recognise you. And I still remember how angry you sometimes made me – you were talented but so lazy.'

He smiled and said, with a touch of irony, 'It never occurred to you that I was tired. You see, I made the beds at the Star Hotel every night.'

Inge blushed. 'Why didn't you tell me?'

'Why didn't you ask?'

She did not answer him, but there had been a reason. That was when her own life had been as bad as it could be, what with the divorce, moving house, child-minding and her little girls crying because they missed their father. Her sense of guilt: what had she done? Her money problems. She had started with the classes for immigrants to earn a little extra, not because teaching them interested her. Though it really was an interesting job or, at least, it should have been . . .

Mira, who had registered the tension round the table, reacted as women always do: she said that they were meant to enjoy having a meal together and that her son was behaving like an oaf. But Inge said his criticism of her had been justified.

Nesto said, 'Maybe you won't believe this but I admired you. There you were, a beautiful Swedish woman, free to manage your own life, self-sufficient and able to support your children.'

If only you'd known, Inge thought. But he went on, 'You read a poem that impressed me very much. There was no photocopier in that place but I wanted to have the poem. I explained to you after the lesson. And you tore out the page, there and then. Tore it out of the book! Remember?'

'Yes, I do.'

'Poetry awaits – all that Man needs . . .'

They recited the remaining lines together:

'. . . is to tell the world he's done great deeds
with greater things still to come . . .

–

but he's no more than a flame in the wind,
a scream at birth and then old wrinkled skin.'

'I can't agree with that,' Mira said.

'Of course not, mother, you're right, as usual,' Nesto said, then turned to Inge. 'You won't believe this, but I carried that poem around in my wallet for years. That is, until the day in the car park outside Auschwitz when I ripped it into tiny pieces and stamped on them and ground them into the pool of my vomit. I had seen the camp and it taught me that nobody should put their trust in dreams and poetry. It's the other way round. The grand beautiful words tempt you then betray you.'

There was silence round the table; they could hear the fluttering flames of the candles. But Nesto wanted to complete what he had begun and went on, emphasising each word: 'Each human being is the sum of his or her own actions. It's true wherever you are, in Nazi Germany or in Chile.'

Inge's mind was a whirlpool of objections, but all she could articulate was: 'What were you doing in Auschwitz?'

Nesto laughed and said, 'My skills include bus-driving. My brother and I are joint owners of a coach – just a minibus, really. We drive people to see what's going on in the rejuvenated countries in eastern Europe – the Czech Republic, Hungary, Poland.' He smiled and said that he was better at finding his way round Poland than Sweden.

'Anyway, one autumn we were taking groups of schoolkids to Auschwitz. It was when people here in Sweden were getting very exercised about neo-Nazis, remember? Some of the district school boards decided that the older pupils should go on a trip to an extermination camp. Teachers came along too – they were meant to control the kids, but you can imagine the scenes in the coach, all fun and games, giggling and pop music and things being thrown about.' He paused briefly. 'The journey home was something else. You should have seen those young people, pale and as quiet as church mice. Many wept. As for me, I went into the camp once. Then I went outside, threw up in the car park and tore up your poem.'

They drank a cup of coffee together before getting up from the table. Mira said that every evening next week she would be at her older son's house to babysit. Keeping the Afros in the greenhouse for another week suited her fine. 'See you next Saturday, then,' she said.

Inge nodded. She shook hands with Nesto, who said, 'Look after Mother. And look out for her too.'

Mira hissed something in Spanish.

'What are you saying?'

Mira pursued her lips but Nesto replied, 'She says that I always show off!' He laughed. After a moment the three laughed together.

When they walked past the car parked in the drive, Nesto said, 'What a heap of old junk you've got there.'

'I know, I know,' Inge said. 'But I can't afford a better one.'

'If you ever have any trouble with it, just give me or my

brother a call. We both know a thing or two about old cars. My brother is pure gold when it comes to engines.' He wrote down a mobile-phone number.

When his car swung out into the street, and she closed her front door, Inge thought, that Mira understood her son well. This was a man who knew how to impress.

CHAPTER 6

For a week Inge was alone in her house. She tried to persuade herself that this was a good thing. She could get on with her work. And she did.

Each day ended in the same way: writing in her diary. And she noticed with surprise that she had more to tell it than ever before. She filled page after page, asked question after question.

Mira said that she refused to remember. It was a source of regret to Inge that she herself had so few memories. Looking at herself in the bathroom mirror in the morning, she thought her eyes were those of a stranger.

She recalled how Mira had recounted the scenes in Graciela's house, describing the women of her childhood with such clarity. Their despair, the demons that rode them. Mira was one of those rare individuals who could fuse observation with understanding.

Then she pondered the story of the seven devils we must all confront before we can meet our guardian angel. Inge had met none of her devils yet. Or had she? Met them and not seen them?

Those damned eyes of hers, devoid of memories.

That Wednesday there was a phone call from her publishers. Could she find time for a meeting with the Danish translator? What about lunch on Thursday, with a meeting beforehand at eleven o'clock?

But on Thursday morning her car would not start. The chill of the night must have killed it. She understood why: it was such a tired old thing.

She did not fancy the idea of calling the garage and having to put up with a group of bored lads laughing at the sad old bag and her clapped-out car.

At the last minute she remembered Nesto. She was tempted. However, she did not dial the long sequence of numbers. Instead she travelled to the centre of town by bus, or buses, actually, because she had to change three times.

She had plenty of time to think.

In the evening she felt tired walking back to her house. Tired and angry. As she walked past the old car she kicked it. Then she went straight to the phone and dialled that mobile number.

He said he could be with her the next day late in the morning.

She would come to learn that sticking to timetables was not his way.

Again she was overwhelmed by his presence as he came into her hall, filling up the doorway. She started telling him about all these changes of bus, but could hear herself whining and tried to apologise: 'Honestly, three changes and two hours each way.'

'I could have driven you,' he said.

She shook her head. As usual, she felt ashamed and cross to be offered help.

It was raining.

'It's much too wet to take the car apart. Come inside and have a cup of coffee. It might dry up later on.'

When they were seated at the kitchen table, she said, 'You seem happy enough living in country where men are not allowed to be macho.' She giggled a little, keen to sound light-hearted.

But letting people near him was not a problem for Nesto and he answered gravely, 'It's been a blow to my sense of identity.'

'Identity?'

'How can you feel male if you're forbidden to behave like a man?' He made a sound like a cock crowing.

Inge laughed but realised that she was getting angry. She wanted to say something like, 'A cock presupposes a flock of scatty hens,' but before she could, he continued, 'Of course, it was wonderful to be here in the beginning. Oh, I remember the summers – the light lingering at night, the forests and the beaches. And the girls, as free as the scenery and as lovely as the nights. All ready to be taken.

'A couple of years passed before I realised that it was in fact the girls who took. They wanted a good time, and when it was over, it was thanks and goodbye. I was like a new, exotic dish on the menu.'

'So you felt exploited, just as women have since time immemorial?'

But he was not listening. He slapped the palm of his hand on the table-top and said, quavering slightly, 'Christ, when

27

I think of my father, who came here and straight away lost his standing. He became a shadow. Mother and we boys would just walk past him, barely noticing him. Of course, now, with hindsight, I can see that we all had much to overcome. Especially Mira. You wouldn't believe me if I told you what she was like when we lived in Chile – submissive and ignorant, listened to mush on the radio while she was ironing and she ironed practically all the time, except when she was tidying.

'And she must have shut her ears whenever the radio broadcast politics. She got the message the day she opened the front door and faced an armoured car full of soldiers with their machine-guns trained on her.'

After this they stayed silent for a long time, then he sipped his coffee and said, 'I never found out how she felt. She withdrew into herself. At the time, my father was away. It was a relief, things were quieter then. But Nana was pale and muted. My sister worried about her. We boys had no idea – it's terrible to think now but for us it was an exciting time, what with the demonstrations and all the trouble in the streets. And then . . . But what happened is something for her to tell. If she ever will.'

It had stopped raining. Inge sat down in front of the computer but did not manage to produce a single sensible sentence.

She went shopping.

When she returned in the afternoon, she found her car in pieces. There was a note on the kitchen table saying that Nesto would be back on Sunday and would bring his brother.

She sighed. Her old Morris was a dead loss. Then she cast

an eye round the kitchen and was surprised at how clean and neat it was.

He had tidied up.

CHAPTER 7

'Mira, it wasn't that you were stupid.'

'You wouldn't know about the connection between ignorance and stupidity.'

'You must have understood something of what was happening.'

'Oh, they carried on all the time, I heard them on the radio – rather like the way they do here, going on about the clash between left and right. None of that seemed any concern of mine.'

'But your husband was a left-wing activist.'

'In Chile, men don't speak to women. If I ever asked him anything, he'd get angry and send me to bed.'

Inge was so astounded she almost dropped the coffee mug. Then she whispered, 'That's what they used to do here with disobedient children.'

'I was terrified of him all the time. Christ, I told you, I only became human after coming to Sweden.'

They sat together silently for a while, watching the children kick a ball around in the yard below.

Finally, Mira said, 'Of course I should've guessed. The food was disappearing from the shops. My husband was away more than ever – he just came and went, was away in the evenings, for whole nights. Meetings, he said. Well, that's what he said to the boys. He felt they'd be better off knowing nothing. He didn't talk to me, but I had to be on hand at night, when he came home hungry and wanted fresh bread and hot tea.'

They were sitting on Mira's balcony. The African lilies in their big pots were lined up on the bench and they had looked at them with pleasure, noting how the plants were stretching towards the light. Now they were drinking coffee, very good strong coffee. Inge said, 'But one day you must have realised how things were?'

'I was going through the gate to collect the mail from the box in the street. Something like a tank was standing there, machine-guns pointing at me. Everything was so silent . . .' She stopped, as if she could still hear the terrible silence.

Then she closed her eyes, as if to avoid having to see. 'So many images come back – try to understand. As a child I played on the banks of river Mapocho and now it was running red with blood. A constant stream of dead bodies came floating along.'

She fell silent, then looked towards the sky and said, 'There are so many images in my mind which seem unreal now.'

Inge said nothing. In the end Mira whispered, 'The thoughts are clotting inside my head. I no longer know what I once saw.'

The cake seemed to grow bigger in Inge's mouth. Mira spoke again: 'The only thing I feel sure I remember right is what happened before my father abandoned us.'

Her face softened. Inge said: 'Can you tell me?'

'My father was a jack-of-all-trades. Sometimes he ran an old lorry. He cultivated marguerites – the yard looked like a meadow. It was covered with flowers that nodded in the wind. I picked them, tied them into bunches and put them into buckets with coloured water. It was all worked out –

so many were to be purple or blue or green. Most were to be red, blood-red. People bought the flowers to make wreaths for the dead.'

She did not speak for a while, then smiled a little and went on: 'And then there were the chickens. Lots. We had sixty hens and, oh, a million chicks. Or that's what I thought when I was five and couldn't count very well. Every morning I had to chop the corn for the chickens to eat. I liked that, all these little balls of fluff trying to get close to me, I had to shoo them away all the time. They were so pretty . . . But they were sold in the market too. And so were the eggs, of course.'

'Where did you live?'

'Workers' quarters in one of the suburbs. Large yards, dusty lanes, everything was made of stone. And the river, it was always there if you sneaked out.'

Suddenly she said, 'No. I have no forests to remember. Only the distant Andes rising above the city smog.'

Her voice had a ring of finality. Inge did not dare mention the daughter and asked instead, 'Why did your father abandon you?'

'I'll let you have a picture of my mother.'

When they parted that afternoon they hugged.

Inge said that Mira was welcome to some of the pink geraniums – she had more than enough, as usual. And Mira said she would come along with José, who was due to check Inge's old car on Sunday morning.

As Inge walked home, the evening was warm and somehow full of promise. Crowds of people were ambling about, their talking and laughing filling the streets with music.

Spring was in the air.

But not even this could make her feel happy.

CHAPTER 8

On Sunday morning, spring really arrived. Not as it usually did, reluctantly, hesitating before each step. No, this time it came in a storm, heralded by thunder and lightning flashes. Inge woke as the first clap shook the walls of her bedroom. Not possible, she said to herself.

For a long while, she stood by the window watching the rainwater washing over the panes. This was no ordinary grey drizzle, but the heavens opening. A benign, warm downpour. It hammered against the roofs and made the earth steam. Best of all, it showed no mercy to the snow. It washed away the dirty drifts still lying on north-facing slopes and showered the rocks clean. The grey granite came to the surface and the flowing water in ditches and gutters sounded like singing.

The dramatic display lasted almost exactly an hour. Then the thunder wandered eastwards over the sea and the sun emerged over the wet earth and dried it. The steam rose into the sky, where it became fresh rain and fell somewhere else. For a moment, there was silence, and then the birds started to sing. Mostly it was piping and chattering from sparrows and tits. But Inge suddenly heard the trills of her blackbirds and thought, This is my reward for feeding them apples all through the winter.

She put on her wellingtons and went out to inspect her garden. There was no question about it: all the scents of spring were rising from the soil, and – just – from snowdrops and crocuses. She stood, in awe, over by the rock-face: only yesterday the bulbs had been struggling through the snow and now their petals were opening towards the sun.

The ash trees on the common stayed tight, unmoved by the miraculous morning. The American sycamore in the neighbours' garden seemed lifeless too, its bare black branches outlined against the sky, but the common sycamores were in bud: soon they would flower, gathering bees with their honeyed scent.

The weeping birch, too, used to be brave and in leaf early. Inge walked into the warmth of the south side of the house to inspect it: there were no little green mouse ears to be seen yet.

It was so warm she had to take off her coat. She stood there for quite some time, wearing only her pyjamas, breathing deeply in the gentle air.

Only after she had finished her yoghurt and moved on to the morning cup of coffee did her thoughts return to what Mira had said of the photo she had been allowed to borrow. It was going to tell her something important. Or was it?

CHAPTER 9

A beautiful woman emerged from the obscurity of the old photo. Her almond-shaped eyes looked into the distance, as if refusing to meet Inge's gaze.

This was odd: people posing for a photograph would normally stare straight into the camera. And the detail lets you know that it was taken in a photographer's studio: the shaded background, her elegant dress, her necklace and the rose on the breast.

Large dark eyes, a little slanted. Were they indignant? Or empty? In any case, they had a faraway expression, as if the present does not matter. Her mouth looked hard, the thin lips closed so tightly that their delicate outline was almost lost. Anger? Fear? She looked as if she had made up her mind and that nothing would ever change it.

Slowly Inge became aware that the picture saddened her. There was a lump in her throat. She could not see why and tried to think of ordinary things, to be curious in a normal way. Mira did not look like her mother. Superficially, the woman in the picture was the more beautiful: her oval face was as perfect as the Virgin Mary's in a medieval icon. She was slender, her nose long and finely chiselled, her posture poised.

Almost everything about Mira was plump. More than once Inge had thought that she had never seen a face as intensely alive: constantly changing, reflecting every feeling. Tightening in anger but never shut off, not even in fury. Most often it was curious. Mira's eyes consumed the world, enjoying each new sight.

Inge studied the picture again and went cold when she imagined what it must have been like to be the child of an ice-queen mother whose gaze was lost in the distance.

Something did not ring true. There was something wrong here, Inge thought. And then: It's just a photo.

This woman was dressed up in her finery because she was going to have her photograph taken. Probably tried to stand very straight in front of the camera. Those compressed lips? Maybe she had bad teeth.

When Inge was tidying up after breakfast, Mira phoned. Her voice was a shriek of delight: 'Have you seen? Here we are, waiting for spring, and what do we get? It's summer now, more than twenty degrees outside.' Her laugh rattled the receiver.

'Yes, I've been round the garden. But I've spent most of the time sitting in the kitchen looking at the photograph of your mother.' Silence. Inge hesitated. What should she say?

Mira broke the silence: 'I understand if it makes you feel sad. She was difficult.'

Another long silence. Finally Inge said, 'I've been wondering how you came to be the way you are.'

'You haven't realised that I am one of those people who's always unsure where to put their foot down next.'

They agreed that there was no time for serious talking that weekend. Practically the entire Narvaes family was turning up to fix the car.

'I'll look after the lunch,' Mira said. 'I'll stop somewhere on the way to your place and buy what's needed.'

'Fantastic.'

Inge took to José at once. A shy warmth was hidden deep behind his eyes. He was a Spaniard, unlike his brother and his mother. He might have come out of a painting by Velázquez.

Inge said thoughtlessly, 'Can you dance flamenco?'

'No, but I'm keen on paragliding.'

Inge was baffled: she had no idea what he's talking about. He misunderstood and said apologetically, 'Only once in while, of course, when I can spare the money.'

He did not share his brother's easy fluency, but tried to describe why he liked gliding – the incredible sense of freedom, the air, the vast space.

Inge sympathised, but wanted to get back to base: 'How do you like living in Sweden?'

He tossed his head proudly, like a true Spaniard: 'I am

Swedish. I did my National Service, two years of commando training in Arvidsjaur.'

'I see,' Inge said, and thought of all the young Swedish men desperate for this placement who had been rejected as unsuitable.

Then Mira's stories about her eldest came suddenly to Inge's mind, stories of the child who would be sitting under her bed, drawing and painting.

They were interrupted when Nesto breezed in, hand in hand with José's little boy.

Inge bent over the child and shook hands. 'My name is Inge Bertilsson and I'm a teacher.'

He answered, as decorously, 'My name is Lars-José and I'm in primary one.'

'Do you like school?'

'Well, it's a bit babyish, really. You see, I could read and write before I started.'

Inge recalled the problems faced by precocious children in Swedish schools, and said, hesitantly, 'It's going to get better later on, don't you think? When the others catch up with you.'

'Daddy says that too. But I have no friends.'

Inge felt chilled, but said truthfully, 'Then we're the same, you and I. When I was a child, I had no friends either.'

'What did you do?'

'I made up stories and had pretend friends and things.'

He nodded. 'I do too.'

By now Mira had climbed out of Nesto's minibus and was dashing along, in her usual style, her hands full of carrier-bags. The little boy started a long eager harangue in Spanish. Mira laughed and translated: 'He says he likes you a lot.'

Then the boy left them to join the men working on the car. Inge followed him and watched for a while, noting that José was shaking his head. This is going to cost, she said to herself, and then: Oh, never mind, what does it matter?

She helped Mira unpack. The little boy came back into the kitchen and told her that Nana liked to be on her own when she was cooking. Mira winked at Inge and laughed when Lars-José explained, 'She gets cross if you try to help her. So I thought you might as well read me a story.'

'But we mustn't stay indoors now when the sun is shining. Come on, let's fix the hammock.'

Inge and the child pushed and pulled the hammock out of the store cupboard and on to the sunny, south-facing patio. It was tricky to get all the poles set up in the right way, but it was finally in place, complete with cushions. Inge was glad she had her collection of fairy-tales and picked one with illustrations by Åke Arenhill. It was a beautiful book, with a cover of red silk and gilt lettering.

'Wow,' said the little boy.

They scanned the book and its many lovely drawings. Then they decided to read the story of Lunkentus. Just as it was getting exciting, the child put up his hand: 'You've got to stop reading now. I want to think about the rest myself.'

Inge was surprised, but also drowsy from the warm sunshine. 'Let's lie back and just think then,' she said, settled into the cushions, pulled him close and started the hammock rocking gently. Both were asleep in seconds, and half an hour later they were woken by Mira's laughter.

'I knew it! I forgot to tell you that Lars-José always wants to finish stories on his own. When he's asleep.'

'Mira, I'd almost forgotten what it's like to hold a child in my arms.'

There was much laughter round the table at lunchtime. Mira was told many times how good her food tasted, how masterfully she combined Swedish and Chilean cooking styles and how nobody anywhere could handle herbs and spices as well as she.

Mira beamed like the sun.

Inge offered wine but neither Nesto nor José drank.

The talk flowed easily, there were stories to tell and more laughter. They told Inge about the only time the family tried to get help from the social services. They laughed in anticipation, it was clearly a family legend. Inge noted this, also that Mira's smile lacked enthusiasm. It was reluctant – even a little ashamed?

'You see, I fell in love,' Nesto said, and Lars-José shouted, 'With an Alfa Romeo!'

'All through my years at school, right up to A levels, I carried on making beds in that hotel. Every morning I walked home in the early hours, and I saw her one very special morning, which I'll never forget.

'*Jesu Christo!* She was gorgeous. She had been damaged in a collision, but it hadn't ruined her beautiful lines. Slipstreams still seemed to flow around her, like gusts in a storm – well, in my imagination.

'My head was bursting with ideas. I'd repair her, make her perfect again. One morning I couldn't resist the temptation. I got off the bus and went into the car park to stand there for something like an hour just looking at her. Then the man who owned her turned up. He'd spotted me from a window in his flat. He said, "She's yours for ten thousand kronor."

'My God, that was a fortune. Still, I had savings. You can guess what happened next. We got a mate to tow the Alfa to our garage and I set to work. José helped me, but it was much more expensive than we'd thought. All the spare parts had to be ordered from Italy. Still, we made it. I took her for a trial run. She was divine. Then somebody in class at school said I had to pay tax. I wouldn't be allowed to drive her without a tax disc. One thousand kronor. I was completely broke. Worse, I had already borrowed money from Mother. I almost wept with disappointment.

'That day I was walking in central Stockholm and happened to see a sign saying 'Social Services'. I remembered that somebody I knew had said that they'd lend you money, if you really needed it. I stepped inside, got myself a queue-slip and finally got to see a guy with a beard. When I told him about the Alfa, his lips seemed to twitch, as if he was about to smile. Then he told me that this was not really a case for Social Services. I said I'd pay him back in a month and he replied, "That's what they all say." Then he started laughing and said, "What the hell? OK."

'I don't know what he'd written on the paper I took to the cashier's counter but I got the money.

'A month later I had enough savings to cover the thousand-kronor loan. I stuffed the note into a jeans pocket and went along to the social-services office. The social worker was on his way out to lunch, but he recognised me. I handed him the note and thanked him for being so helpful. He stuttered objections. He couldn't take cash, he said. Then he went with me to a post office and arranged to send the social services a giro for the amount. We went to a pizzeria afterwards, had pizza and beer. He kept laughing all the time. I remember thinking that he was unusually jolly for a Swede. We still meet for a beer now and then, at least a couple of times a year.'

Inge laughed heartily and happily. She felt proud of the Swedish bureaucrat.

After the coffee they got together in her study to talk business. On the desk lay the photo of Mira's mother. José raised an eyebrow and looked quizzical. He said, 'She was a difficult woman.'

There was something final in his tone, but Nesto said, 'I loved her.'

José shrugged wearily, this seemed to touch an old wound. Then he turned to Inge and said that they could find her a small car for eight or ten thousand kronor. Could she raise this amount?

Yes, she could. 'But is it possible to get a decent car for so little?'

'Yes, no problem', the brothers said, practically in unison. 'Second-hand, lots of miles on the clock, but in good nick.' And they went on: 'It'll go like clockwork once we've finished with it.'

Only when the family had left did it occur to her that she had forgotten to ask how much they were going to charge her for all the work they had done on her old car. 'Never mind,' she said aloud to herself.

But she wrote in her diary: 'This summer looks like being a lean time.' And then the thought raced into her head: second-hand car dealers – sharks.

Immigrants.

She felt ashamed afterwards – so deeply ashamed that she had to do something. She started washing up. Not such a bad idea. She applied herself to the task energetically. Tidied the kitchen.

She even considered hoovering, but decided against it. That night, she slept well.

CHAPTER 10

Mira, however, had a disrupted night. Fear screamed to her that this friendship must end.

What had Inge been saying about the photo of Mira's mother? The question went round and round in her head, but not the answer. All she could hear was the sadness in her friend's voice. That bloody woman was exposing her, tearing her apart.

She tried to make God understand this, but He did not relent. 'Have some sense,' He said. Then He comforted her by pointing out that she had had a lovely day and her sons had been a credit to her, that she had every reason to be pleased and proud.

Yes, of course, she agreed. 'But you don't understand,' she said to God. 'Inge is as cunning as a snake. She no longer asks me straight questions. Instead she crawls about, round and round, sneaking up on me, black and dangerous. She's not told me one thing about herself. And now the poison is seeping out of all my wounds.'

'They never healed,' God said.

But Mira was no longer paying attention to Him. 'How can I defend myself against a well-meaning Swede – who understands nothing?'

Weeping made her feel a little better, and she was able to sleep. But she woke suddenly and her heart was beating too fast. God was silent now, He was not within reach. But there was somebody else . . . Who?

She could not deny his presence for long. It was her boy, her first-born. They shot him and killed him. His body was thrown on to a lorry and driven to the river.

'Oh, Javi,' she said. Agony filled her, almost broke open her ribcage.

Then anger came to her rescue and she took the chance to scold him: 'What were you doing outside in the streets, you idiot? You knew about the curfew, you told me yourself that they shot at people from the helicopters that patrolled the city. And there you were, hanging out with Guille in his fucking car.'

She stopped for a moment. Javi wouldn't understand the Swedish swear-words. But he answered her: 'It was the car, Nana, Guille's new car . . . When he said to come along for a ride I couldn't say no. I remember we told each other that the helicopter crews wouldn't hammer the cars. And they didn't. It was an armoured car that got us.'

She wanted to ask him a thousand questions. When he died, had he been in pain? Did he know that they had become refugees? Did he know anything of the land they had fled to?

But even as she asked the first question, he had disappeared.

She was soaked in sweat. She turned on her lamp, got out of bed, turned on all the lights in the flat. Her teeth were chattering. She went into the bathroom and stood under the shower for a long time.

Her boy, her beautiful boy. His smile was a delight – José had it too, but showed it only rarely and quickly, as if he was ashamed of it. But, then, José was harder to understand, more withdrawn – a more complex person. Not like Javi, whose charm was effortless and who had been given joy as a gift at birth.

'Oh, God,' she said. 'Only you know how much I loved that child.'

But God was not listening and she thought that maybe He, too, needed His sleep. She got into bed and pulled the blankets decisively round her shoulders.

Then she thought that since the boy had come during the night, the girl might come as well.

'No,' she cried.

Afterwards she must have fallen asleep.

When she woke she felt convinced suddenly that the reason Otilia had not come was that she was not dead. She must have been one of those who 'disappeared'. The idea terrified Mira.

CHAPTER 11

Inge had slept well, a good long night's sleep. She had woken to see the sun pouring in through her bedroom window like a river of gold and felt a pang of pure joy. Truly, it was springtime.

Standing at the kitchen door, she watched the first starling of the year. She wanted to hold it in her hands and speak to it, telling it how grateful she was that it had battled its way here through snow and rain. Northwards, always northwards, with the wind against it. Mile after mile. You brave little bird, she wanted to say.

But where was the rest of the flock?

Then she spotted it, a scattering of birds on the lawn, their coats glowing like brown pearls, speckled with black and white.

She chopped bread and cheese for them, opened the door and listened, enchanted, to the fluttering noise of the whole flock taking off and flying to the trees on the common. As silently as she could she walked barefoot into the garden and spread her welcome-home breakfast over the lawn. She then stood absolutely still just inside the kitchen doorway and watched the birds as they pecked at their meal

Just as she finished making the coffee, the phone rang. That's odd, she said to herself. Who would phone before eight on a Monday morning?

A voice speaking English asked if she was prepared to pay for the call. Inge agreed happily, but then felt anxious. Why had they phoned at this time of day? She hoped nothing was wrong.

But on the phone her two daughters chatted easily across each other: oh, yes, they were fine! The daffodils were in flower in London.

Britta said, 'We thought it would be a good idea to call you and let you know something. We went to see Daddy and Marilyn yesterday. He wasn't there and she said they're going to get a divorce.'

Inge stood there in silence. Her hand holding the receiver was sticky with sweat.

'It seems she's had a hard time, mostly, and the children aren't very happy either. We never told you before, but he's really . . . well, dependent on alcohol.'

Inge did not say anything.

'Marilyn's got her library job back. She's going to sell the house. The boys will stay with her parents in Yorkshire this summer. It's the real countryside, you know.'

Inge still did not – could not – say anything.

'Mummy, are you there?'

She managed to say yes.

'We thought you'd better know. For one thing, there's always the risk that he will turn up at your place.'

'No!' Inge almost shouted now.

'Mummy, please, he isn't dangerous or anything.'

'Yes!' Her voice was still very loud. 'He's a danger to me. I don't want him, he frightens me . . . I'll move out.'

'But, Mummy . . .'

Inge was weeping now, snivelling into the receiver. Between sobs, she stammered that she'd phone back – soon. And then she hung up.

A quarter of an hour later she rang back and was able to ask: 'What's happened, exactly?'

'We don't know much. Marilyn spoke mostly of how he was drinking a lot and could become very nasty, both to her and the boys. He's been sacked from his job. Nobody knows where he is.'

'Has he found a new woman?'

'Marilyn doesn't think so. It was she who said he might go back to you. But, Mummy, listen, there's no need to be scared of him. If he turns up give him a cup of coffee and let him talk to you for a while.'

She could not let them know the real situation, so she stayed silent.

Finally Britta said, 'You come here, Mummy. Book a flight straight away. Ingrid's exams will be over by May, then she can go home with you.'

'Thank you,' Inge said, and started crying again. 'I'll phone you tonight, I need to think . . .'

She went to bed, felt cold, and curled up under the duvet. A little later she got up, went round her house and checked all the locks, switched off all the lights, closed all the windows.

I must be mad, she said to herself.

She settled her accounts, called her publishers to let them know she was taking a short holiday and then Nesto to say that the car could wait, she had to go to London. She contacted a friend to ask if they might go and see a film together, but the friend was already busy. She phoned Mira at work. She had intended to ask if she could drop in later on, but what she said was: 'May I sleep over at your place?'

'Of course.'

She went to the day-nursery where Mira worked and got the key to her flat. Once there, settled on the sofa in the sitting room, Inge's heart finally slowed. She sank deeper and deeper into sleep.

When Mira woke her she could say, almost with a smile, 'I've got to be crazy.'

Mira handed her a large brandy. 'Drink this.'

'Thank you.' And then Inge told the story of how her ex-husband had been thrown out by his English wife and might appear, any time now, at her house.

'What's so scary about that?'

She could say it then: 'I still love him.'

Mira snorted and said, 'I'm going to make us some coffee and sandwiches. You haven't eaten for ages.'

Sitting at the kitchen table, neither of them spoke. Not for a long time.

Finally Mira started telling Inge about last night. About

46

her dead son, who had come to visit her, and about her daughter, who never came. And about the conclusion she had reached: that the girl was alive. She must be among the disappeared.

'That's almost worse,' she said, tears pressing painfully behind her eyelids. Inge wept openly.

'During the night I was so angry with you – you and your questions, which forced me to remember.'

Inge wanted to defend herself, to tell Mira that nobody should try to escape their past and that, anyway, she hadn't intended . . . But she said nothing.

Mira went on, 'I was determined to ask you about yourself and make you tell me. Inge, you're so secretive. But then I thought you would just use many many words, probably none of them true. I had thought about asking you why you divorced but you would have had all the usual Swedish answers ready for me, about how hard it had been, what with children and work and cooking and cleaning, and how he had been expecting his shirts ironed and his children looking pretty, tucked up in bed and preferably asleep.'

'You're right – or were,' Inge said. 'That's what you would have been told yesterday.' She appealed to Mira, 'You must understand, I believed that myself and, anyway, it's true too.'

'But not the whole truth?'

'No.'

'This is what makes life so complicated for you Swedes. You always want explanations, to understand. The thing is, there's no understanding this goddamn life.'

They sat in silence again. Then Mira smiled and said, 'Can you see God's finger?'

47

'I think I can sense it,' Inge answered fearfully.

More silence.

'How do you picture your daughter when you think about her?'

'Maybe drifting about in the country, her mind gone. I'm sure there's no hospital left to care for Chile's mad people any more. She might be one of the whores in Santiago. Or she might have got married to one of Pinochet's thugs and be going to Junta parties. She is very beautiful, like her grandmother.'

Mira's agony was almost tangible.

'Now it's your turn to have a brandy,' Inge said. It was hard to make Mira drink. She almost had to force the brandy on her friend. 'There must be a way of finding out about that girl of yours, if she's still alive. There have to be organisations, people who have got together to investigate. Amnesty might know. You write to relatives in Santiago, don't you?'

'They'd never dare ask about Otilia. These are dangerous questions . . .'

Mira began to weep. 'It's the brandy. It's making my brain feel all fuzzy,' she said apologetically.

'Good,' Inge said calmly. 'That means you'll get some sleep tonight.'

Then she said goodbye. She said she would not be staying the night.

On her way home, Inge thought carefully about what she would say if Jan was sitting waiting for her on the door-step. She would pretend not to have heard anything about his divorce and merely ask what he was doing there. He might say that he wanted to come in and talk for a while and, if so, she would answer that she was in too much of a hurry, that she was about to finish a book. He would accuse her of never having any time to spare for him. But she would not argue, just tell him they had nothing to say to each other any more.

He was not sitting on the steps to her house, or course.

The air was stale and she opened doors and windows to create a through-draught.

While she was unlocking everything, she felt ashamed, like a scolded dog. She had lost her grip. She had behaved hysterically.

She phoned her daughters and said she was sorry. 'I cannot think what got into me.'

'But you are coming on Wednesday, aren't you?'

'Yes, of course. As we agreed.'

'Good. We'll talk then. You can make us understand.'

That means I've only twenty-four hours to make myself understand, Inge thought afterwards. At that moment she seemed to hear Mira laugh.

CHAPTER 12

Can love be, as the Greeks believed, embodied in a god who shoots arrows that make life glow? Or is it just another great myth? Perhaps both are true. But the meanings are profoundly different.

The god with his bow and arrow was the offspring of two opposing forces: his father was Ares, god of war and his mother Aphrodite, goddess of passion. He carried complex and fateful messages.

Myth is the creation of man, a response to the inexplicable.

Why did it hurt so much, after all these years? Whatever could have led her to tell Mira she loved him still, to this day?

She tried to re-create his image in her mind. Coarsened now, an alcoholic. A pain in her stomach doubled her over. She had to go to the lavatory. She saw her pale face in the mirror and told it: Don't lose control again.

But, oh, Christ, Jan, the pity of it.

She saw her father's chiselled face, his kind eyes. His soft hands caressing her. His joyless smiles. He used to say that she was the only thing that made his life worthwhile. For as far back as she could remember, she had been trying to protect him from her mother's anger. There were times when Inge had managed to silence her. But she could never really make it up to her father. The child kept failing.

The quarrels – all these drawn-out, terrible quarrels, which scared her out of her mind. She would hide in the coat cupboard and clamp her hands over her ears when her parents started carving up each other's worth as a human being.

He was a coward, screeched her mother.

That's right, he'd always been too weak, her father agreed.

The quarrels stopped when she was twelve years old. Her father told his daughter proudly than he had found another woman. He was happy now.

Christ, how she had missed him after the divorce.

The girl felt so alone.

Every night, her mother wept in bed, until one morning she remembered that she had a child and stopped weeping.

It was too late by then, of course, but with time, mother and daughter became friends. They never spoke about the past.

Inge's mother found touching people difficult. She could not handle words at all. Her idea of bringing up her child was to impart to her a pride in herself. The little girl responded, anxious that she might lose her mother too.

She did well at school: previously undistinguished, she was now top of the class. She grew up to be pretty. Then she went to university and pleased her mother by leaping one academic hurdle after another.

Later in life, when she herself had been left alone with her children, Inge thought more about her mother. She recalled her strength and her hard life. She had had no education, so in the evenings she worked as an office cleaner, and in the mornings she scrubbed the communal stairs in blocks of flats.

Inge's father provided not a penny in support.

The decision had been that the child would visit her father every second weekend. She never liked his new home and one day she realised that his new wife could be as furiously angry as his old one. Violent quarrels seemed always to lie in wait at the kitchen table. They would break out the moment the girl had said goodbye and left.

There was a new child, a whining baby boy. Her visits grew less frequent. She would never forget the last one. That had been the first time she saw her father as he was. 'He's a martyr,' said the new wife. She knew more words than Inge's mother.

Inge carefully observed her father's finely proportioned face. The dead smile came and went, mechanically and pointlessly. The same applied to the tears, which so often filled his eyes. Her mother had been right, he was a sap. But the child had been right as well: he was pitiful.

She never visited again.

But she did not stop loving him. She still loved him. He was in long-term care now and she went to see him once a month. Being cared for suited him. Finally he was getting his due. Here at last were plenty of patient women, unbearably kind and apparently always willing to listen.

His son, Inge's half-brother, had fled to Australia. He never even sent a Christmas card.

Inge wanted to halt the flow of images. She walked about in the warm night air and breathed deeply. But her mind was still racing. That's how I am, she thought. No need for a god to turn up and shoot at me with a bow and arrow, I was ready to fall for Jan anyway.

The thought was hurtful: she felt that she had once owned a splendid thing then crushed it.

Now the images changed.

To lie in Jan's arms, the wonderful time they had together, exploring each other slowly and tenderly, discovering new surprises. Their bodies had been filled with joy. The body contains a capacity for happiness that transforms the world outside into glittering reflections.

Jan gave me my body and I'll probably never experience anything more important. He gave me all my sensuality – the use of my senses to see, taste, listen and enjoy.

It was almost midnight when she went to bed. She stretched and told herself that she must get some sleep. But sleep failed her and instead she was gripped by lust. As so often, she hugged her large pillow. Afterwards, she cried.

CHAPTER 13

In the morning, Inge felt relief as she locked up her house and went to leave the keys with a next-door neighbour.

'I'll go round every evening and check that things are all right,' said Kerstin. 'You know, just in case. Not that anything ever happens here.'

She's right, Inge thought. Nothing happens here. Footsteps on the drive had woken her at four in the morning. Then, a thump at the letterbox. The paper-boy. But Inge had had palpitations and found it hard to go back to sleep.

She had phoned Mira early on. Her friend's voice sounded deep and hoarse. 'I've found out that there's an organisation in London, set up by refugees from Chile, to trace people who disappeared during the coup,' Inge said.

Mira did not answer for quite a while. Finally, she said, 'I must have time to think. And talk with José and Nesto.'

'I understand, of course. I'll call you from London in a few days' time.'

Inge had told the image in her bathroom mirror in a loud, angry voice, 'You have nothing to fear except your own weakness.' The reflection agreed. When her features had relaxed, she had smiled at herself but noted that her smile was as joyless as her father's. She looked like him, everyone had told her so as she grew up.

But no, not this. 'I'm no useless sap,' she said, and once more her reflection nodded in agreement.

In the plane, she thought of her daughters waiting at Heathrow airport, a little alarmed by their mother's reaction. Concerned for her too, because they were so used to her being in control.

And there they were! Both blondes, with finely drawn features, wide foreheads, straight noses and proudly poised heads. They looked like their mother. Britta alone had something of Jan, a big laughing mouth and very white teeth.

They were both talking at the same time during the long journey by bus into central London. There to study, they were staying in a cheap guest-house. The worn-looking woman who ran the place welcomed Inge and said that the usual room was ready for her. None of the three women was hungry, because they had a long-standing agreement to eat beforehand, Inge on the plane and the girls in an airport cafeteria.

Inge tried to convince them that she had no idea what had happened to her when they told her of Jan's divorce. She felt much calmer now. 'This morning I was talking to my own reflection in the mirror, saying that I've got nothing to fear except my own weakness.'

'Does he still make you feel weak after all these years?'

Inge confessed, 'When I was at my most hysterical, I told a friend I loved him.'

'Is that true?'

'No, I don't think so. I've had a couple of nights to ponder it.'

'What was your conclusion?'

'Well, oddly enough, I kept thinking about my father.'

'Grandfather?'

'Yes.' She told them of the images that had come and gone during that first night, and about the links she had discovered.

Later, Britta remarked on how odd it was that it should be Jan's divorce that made them recall and rethink events and relationships, although on the face of it his divorce was no business of theirs.

'We've been thinking a lot about how we used to be really angry with you for throwing him out. We'd long for him to come back. He'd be noisy and make us laugh and lift us high in the air. We thought it was awful to have to move out to Nowhere Land – into that tiny terraced house, but that it would be such fun to go to London and visit him.'

'I realise all that,' Inge said, and her sudden sense of guilt was like a kick in the belly.

But the girls kept talking, still at the same time. 'Listen, Mummy, there's lots you don't know. Like, the English visits were no fun at all. Marilyn was kind and tried her best to make us feel at home, but Daddy . . . Daddy didn't take any notice of us. He didn't seem to care. Never asked how we were getting on, what we were doing at school, stuff like that. And never told us anything about himself. It took some time to sink in. The dream of our wonderful daddy died the death slowly, during the winter months in Sweden. Do you remember when we refused to go to England?'

Inge remembered well enough when the children had come home looking gloomy and she had heard them crying in the evenings.

'Why didn't you tell us then that he was a selfish bastard?'

'Oh, for heaven's sake,' Inge said, paused, then went on angrily, 'Would you have believed me?'

'Maybe not. But at least we'd have had something to hold on to when we discovered what he was really like. You've been so pathetically loyal. Every which way, all the time.'

Inge said nothing.

'He didn't care for his new children, the boys, either,' Britta said. 'Marilyn's had a hard time for many years, but lately it's been worse than ever. I don't understand how she put up with it. When we talked to her about it, she shrugged her shoulders and asked why we didn't ask you the same question.'

Inge said nothing, but Britta would not give in. 'Mummy, how did you put up with it for so long?'

Inge spoke at last and all three could hear how weary she felt: 'I was so uncertain.' But then her voice became stronger and harsher: 'You see, it's essential to hate. I find hatred difficult. Somehow I perceive it as forbidden.' Her gaze shifted to the ceiling. 'I was uncertain about everything, but above all about money – how to keep the home going. Pride was a problem too. It was difficult to leave a university post to take up a full-time job as a suburban school-teacher. Like I said, hatred is essential. And one must be enormously strong. Achieving that took time for me. And then, after the divorce and just as things were falling into place, grief struck me. You were not the only ones who longed for Jan.'

They sat together in silence for a long time. Ingrid cried, but Britta tried to change the subject. 'We went to see Marilyn because we thought she might need help with moving out. Her brothers were there, which put up a barrier between us. So "typically English", you know? We got really cross and that made us slave away like anything – not that it did us any good.'

'I thought they became a bit friendlier,' Ingrid said.

She had gone to get a bottle of beer and Inge drank thirstily. She had forgotten how nice English beer was.

'Are his whereabouts still unknown?'

'That's right. Marilyn and her brothers are trying to trace him. They're very insistent that it's their problem, not ours. We're grown-up now and have no claim on him. As if we ever did.'

Britta opened another bottle of beer. Inge drank some more, not noticing that her daughters were exchanging anxious glances.

'There's one unpleasant thing left to tell you. When Jan disappeared, he took the family savings with him, all the money Marilyn had been putting away to see the boys through school.'

Inge's face turned a fiery red, but the anger she felt was as cold as ice.

'Mummy, why were you so frightened that time on the phone? Were you feeling all alone in the wilderness?'

'Not at all. I'm used to being on my own.' She examined her feelings but ended up shaking her head. Loneliness had had nothing to do with her strange reaction. After a while she smiled and said, 'Anyway, something nice has happened to me. I've become friendly with a family from Chile. You know, they really make me look at things and see them in a new way.' Then she started telling them of how she'd met Mira in the garden centre and how well they had got on, talking about the African lilies. And about Nesto the Indian and José the Spaniard, who had promised to do something about her car.

Her daughters listened, staring at her with round baffled eyes. When she stopped for breath and more beer, both girls roared with laughter.

Inge watched in surprise. Finally Ingrid pulled herself together enough to say: 'You won't believe this, Mummy. You see, we've got a Chilean secret as well – the Indian variety, young and good-looking. His name is Fernando Larraino and he's called Nano. Britta and he are in love.'

Inge's laughter almost choked her and she said solemnly, 'God's finger. Again.'

Ingrid asked if she'd become religious. 'Just a tiny bit,' Inge said. 'It's Mira's fault.'

'Is she a Catholic?'

'Not really, she's herself. She talks to God quite often and some nights she encounters the spirits of the dead.'

Inge decided to ignore the girls' astonishment. She said she wanted to meet Britta's friend and talk to him.

'I'll phone and invite him for dinner,' Britta said. Her face went pink with pleasure.

Nano was quite different from her Swedish Chileans. True, his skin, too, was a shade of honey and his cheekbones were high and prominent. But everything about him spoke of upper-class style and poise. He moved gracefully and, when he was introduced to Inge, spoke easily with just the right amount of charm. His English, with its slightly nasal drawl, hinted at an expensive public-school education.

Inge tried hard to ignore her prejudices.

He had brought his car, he said, and had booked a table at an Indonesian restaurant. It would be a pleasure to invite his Swedish friends to dinner.

'Thanking you most humbly,' Ingrid said, and her mother heard the sarcasm. So did Nano. He blushed a little.

This is not going entirely smoothly, Inge thought, and looked at Britta, who seemed not to have noticed. 'My mother would like to talk to you alone for a moment,' she said, and at once the boy seemed to drop his guard. He looked young and vulnerable. Inge liked him better now.

They went to her room and she immediately began to

tell him about her friend in Sweden and the friend's daughter, who had disappeared. Was it true that there was a London organisation that investigated such cases?

He sighed with relief and then said that he himself was not particularly engaged in Chilean problems. However, his mother was and she had many friends with the same convictions. Also, she was a lawyer. He would arrange for them to meet.

Inge beamed at him, but said, 'Please, do not mention this to the others yet.'

'It'll remain our secret,' said the young man, and lightly kissed her cheek.

CHAPTER 14

The next morning Inge was on her own. Her daughters had left for college and she intended to indulge herself with a long walk in Kew Gardens. Thousands of daffodils and other spring flowers would be in bloom.

But she had barely got dressed when the phone rang.

'Matilde Larraino here. I believe you would like to ask me some questions?'

'That's right.'

'Let's meet for lunch today.'

'I'm really grateful.'

They agreed a time and a place. Inge rang Mira at work. Yes, they'd been talking it over and had decided to give it a try. Inge wrote down the girl's full name and date of birth, and the address of where they had been living. She studied what she had written before putting the piece of paper away in her handbag. The girl had been born in 1961; she had been thirteen when she was raped and fourteen when she disappeared.

She hailed a taxi and the driver manoeuvred skilfully through the traffic to the modest restaurant where Matilde was waiting. Much later, Inge would spend time trying to remember how the other woman had looked at this first encounter. Beautiful, of course, and smartly dressed in a tailored grey suit with pearls at her throat. All this Inge had expected. It was something else that fascinated her so completely that her English was quite shaky at first.

'I mustn't stare,' she told herself. But when the waiter turned up and Matilde got involved in discussing the menu, Inge had a chance to observe her. Brown eyes, so dark the pupil was scarcely visible. Large round spectacles. Chestnut hair, cut so that it followed the shape of her head like a tight-fitting cap. Pale, smooth skin, just a few wrinkles at the corners of her eyes.

Life had surely been kind to her. She looked so untroubled.

When Matilde had ordered, she told Inge that she thought Britta such a likeable girl and that the young people's love for each other was a pleasure to see. 'We'll become members of the same family.'

This astonished Inge, who had not yet thought that far ahead. Then she nodded and said something about today's young people, how they insisted on finding their own way and how she thought this was a good thing.

Matilde answered that for her part she found it difficult to understand the modern way of being in love. She said it was reasonable that there would be many affairs of the heart in a person's life. 'But real love, no, only once.'

Inge looked taken aback, and Matilde said, 'You must

think me an utter romantic. But I'm in a position to know, believe me.'

'Then I'll just have to accept what you say,' Inge said, and they smiled at each other for the first time.

As they ate lemon sole with avocado sauce and drank a glass of white wine, the restaurant filled up. The roar of conversation was such that they found it hard to carry on talking.

'What were your plans for today?'

'A springtime walk in Kew Gardens.'

'Let me join you. I can take the afternoon off.'

The got into a tube train, and an hour later found themselves seated on a bench in the park, shaded by a beech tree covered with new leaves, and surrounded by a sea of tulips.

Inge spoke of Mira and her sons. 'She seemed so open and approachable. All I wanted was to find out about her. I had no idea how much pain my questions would cause her.'

'It was probably not so much your questions but the way you were coming so close. Is she bitter?'

'No, she seems either very happy or very angry, and always curious. She wants to know everything, to learn all the time. She works at her new country, hammers its language and customs into her mind. No day seems to pass without her thinking up new theories about the Swedes and why we behave as we do.'

'Is she critical?'

'Well, she can be. She's kind of . . . explosive. It takes just one second and then she's in a towering rage. When it's over, she laughs at herself.'

'I recognise all this. Live in the present, grab what you can from life. The past didn't happen or, at least, it's dead and buried. Do you see what I mean?'

'I think so.'

'It helps a great deal to be curious about one's new world. Besides, curiosity is useful when immigrants are fighting for survival – coping with never-ending toil to learn a new language, find a job and get educated.'

Matilde looked out over the flower-beds, breathed in the scents, then said, 'I find it so painful to think of your friend. She had left her child in hell and the sudden insight into this was forced on her. Mother of God. It's so hard.'

Matilde's eyes were full of tears as she continued, 'There's another explanation to that loss of memory. I'm sure you're aware of it. It's shame. People who have been subjected to the worst humiliations feel ashamed. Mira has kept silent for a long time, not just because it hurts her to remember but also because she's ashamed. I know. I, too, have been raped and tortured.'

Inge took a deep breath and Matilde went on, 'We're alike, your friend and I. Can you see that?'

Inge thought first then answered as she saw it: that although there were similarities, there were also differences.

'Mira is not as . . . civilised as you are. Class is like nationality, it puts a stamp on people,' she said.

Matilde nodded and said she understood very well what Inge was saying.

Inge blushed. 'I do try to suppress this habit I have of hanging on to middle-class prejudices.'

'And I try to suppress my habit of identifying myself with the upper classes.'

Now they could laugh together.

A class of schoolchildren tramped past their bench and the voices of the children drowned the birdsong.

When they had gone, Matilde continued, 'I grew up in Santiago, but never got to know the city. I knew twenty-odd luxurious rooms and the large park outside. It sheltered me from reality. We had to speak English at dinner, because my father regarded Spanish as the language of the ill-educated, of dreamers and women. Well, at least in Chile, where he felt the language had got out of hand – it had become wild, exaggerated and somehow part of all kinds of magical beliefs. English, on the other hand, he saw as exercise for the brain. It would help us think in a measured, critical way.'

'He wasn't entirely wrong, was he?'

'I suppose not. Anyway, I love Chilean Spanish – it's a language that allows one to be open and emotional.

'There are more things I'd like you to know about my home. For instance, it was crawling with servants, people whose presence seemed as natural to us as the air we breathed. None of us really thought of these gentle, shadowy beings as real people. The poor were out of reach. They got these shirts my mother spent her time making. Is all this hard for you to understand?'

'It is.'

'Actually, it's hard for me too.'

'Maybe differences in level become indistinguishable from a really great height,' Inge said. 'I suppose that's how it must be for God – that's why we're all equal in his eyes.'

'Is that a joke?'

Inge could hear how shocked Matilde was and answered, 'Of course.'

A mother and her children strolled past, accompanied by two large dogs. Matilde sat rigid. When they were alone again, Inge asked, 'But how could someone with your background become an enemy of the military dictators?'

'At first, I was not the slightest bit politically aware. But then I encountered love – great, blessed and accursed love,'

Matilde said, with a passion that startled Inge. She told Inge that she went to university to read law when she was nineteen, in spite of her father's reservations. Her mother had supported her, pointing out that now a daughter had the same right to a good education as a son. Her father had argued that Matilde had a secure future already set up for her. She was beautiful and had had lessons in both French conversation and piano-playing. Above all, she was wealthy.

'So, you see, I was quite a catch in the marriage stakes. Surprisingly, one of my uncles came to my mother's aid and in the end Father gave in. After all, a couple of years at university could hardly harm my prospects.

'The university turned out to be a hotbed of revolutionary politics. Suddenly, I was part of a world that was alive with anger and rebelliousness. I listened and took it all in – oh, how I listened and learnt. And observed. Coming home in the afternoons, I was able to see things in new light. I saw my maid, our gardener and the old cook, and I felt ashamed. But I did not dare speak to them. I stayed silent at home, just I was silent at university. But I had trouble sleeping at night.

'Then one day I met Pedro. At first it was just our eyes that met. There are no words to describe what happened to me in that moment. The next day I went with him to his rented room in one of the slum quarters. Even now, I remember every second of what we did together in his narrow bed.

'He loved me. But his true passion was justice.

'He was serious about the task of making me see reality. We played truant from lectures and walked through a Santiago I had never known. There were thousands of unemployed, thrown out of their jobs in the saltpetre mines in the north, and living in endless, hopeless suburban settlements. They were filthy, always close to starvation – the eyes of the children, hungry and begging, were the worst thing.

'I marched at Pedro's side in wild demonstrations. Mother said that Father would have a stroke if he ever found out. But he never did, because he was away in England on business. When he came home, another kind of catastrophe had struck his family. His lovely daughter was pregnant.

'Without a moment's hesitation, my Father said, "You must have an abortion." I said, "Never." He asked, "Who's the parent?" and I replied, "I won't tell you." And I smiled when I imagined introducing Pedro to my family. The revolutionary with his long bushy beard and hair, wearing his filthy coat and miners' boots.

'My father was shouting at me, saying that I was ruining my family's good name and I shouted back that worse things than a scandal would happen to them soon.

' "What do you mean?"

' "The revolution!"

'He almost hit me then. Later on, my mother told me that he had started shifting investments abroad.

'When the whole country was getting ready for the great election, I was hidden away in the house of country cousin. She was a widow, a kind woman. I always liked her and it was a happy time. The child was growing inside me. Sometimes Pedro came to me at night. He was the leader of a revolutionary group and felt sure that the left would win the election. But he did not believe that the new government would be able to survive. "The capitalists are planning to sabotage any reforms that the government might propose."

'He was right, as it turned out.

'Anyway, to cut a long story a bit shorter, I gave birth to my baby boy on the night that the victory celebrations of the left seemed to touch the sky over Santiago.

'Six months later I returned to the city. Something strange happened then, when I was back with my family. My father came to love my child, his first grandchild, and a boy. A splendid little chap, my father said. He had the family looks on the male side, like my grandfather and a bit like my uncle too. The eyes, the quick mind. Nobody mentioned Pedro. It was only I, still meeting my lover on rare nights, who knew that my little boy was the image of the revolutionary.'

Evening had arrived in the park. A breeze stirred the branches of the trees and suddenly the two women realised they were chilly. Matilde was concerned that telling her life story had been an imposition, but Inge urged her to continue. 'Another time,' Mathilde said.

Inge realised then that her new friend was tired – tired and profoundly saddened. 'I feel I've done to you what I did to Mira,' Inge said. 'I've forced you to remember.'

'There's a difference. I want to remember, I want to tell my story, to repeat it and try to see it in a new light.'

They hailed a taxi and got in. Then Matilde said, without looking at Inge, 'When I arrived in England, they did something that was almost worse than everything else that had happened to me. It was so humilating. I was taken into hospital for a hysterectomy. They had to remove my womb. During the torture, I'd been raped so many times – and Pinochet's demons had trained dogs to enter women. Oh, God, the shame of it, when I had to tell the English doctors what had happened to me.'

66

CHAPTER 15

Mira paced up and down, all night long, night after night. She counted her steps all the way through the kitchen and the sitting room, the bedroom and the hall.

Her conversations with God grew more intense and often ended with conspiratorial deals: 'If only You would . . . then I promise . . .'

She felt silly afterwards.

God did just one thing for her. In spite of the warm spring weather, she caught a cold. She had never been ill enough to miss a single day's work, but she was told to stay at home rather than risk infecting the children at the nursery. This time she failed to spot the finger of God. She certainly wanted no more time to think or remember.

Now the images kept forcing themselves on her.

Santiago. The howling in the streets, the fear.

And . . .

No.

Then Otilia and all the things that might have happened to her. She could picture clearly the whores of Santiago and their pimps. She remembered wondering about these women and how they could bear it all, how they endured just one night. 'Not that, not that, dear Lord,' she prayed.

Other memories came of her little girl when the world was still normal. She had been the most beautiful and sweet-natured of all Mira's children. She had been sweet, as sweet as honey, and her skin had glowed like silk.

She searched for a Swedish word to suit her girl. I know they have a good one, she said to herself. Finally it came to her. 'Fair.' That's how they said it, with a drawling soft sound in the middle. Otilia was fair, the fairest ever.

'Dear Lord,' she said, to the bedroom ceiling, 'why could You not have let her die?'

Perhaps she had survived the torture and married someone, maybe a farm-worker from the southern valleys where great estates sprawled, rich in land and power.

Mira was looking for comfort, but what little she found could not last. To be a farm-worker's wife was a fate she wouldn't wish on her worst enemy: a child born every year, a husband who beat you and then, of course, that stinking rich landowner, who'd rape any reasonable-look-ing woman.

And Otilia was beautiful, like her grandmother.

Her grandmother had noticed it: 'She looks like me,' she had said. 'Poor child.'

For once, Mira had spoken up in the presence of the old woman: 'Why poor?'

'It's a dreadful fate.'

Suddenly Mira found she was crying for her mother, who had been sent from Santiago every summer to stay with relatives on an estate in the south. They had been little more than slaves.

I think I know what happened to you.

Mira went to bed early but could not sleep. 'It's the cough,' she told herself. Her cold felt like a great lump that had stuck in her throat.

Inge, now. She spent a long time raging against Inge. When José came to look after her, she was fuming with anger at her friend, who had been interfering with things that were none of her business. And raked up what had been old and forgotten.

This made him angry in turn. He told her that sooner or

later she had to face the truth. She said he understood nothing; he replied that, on the contrary, it was she who had failed to see.

'What in God's name do you mean?'

'People cannot shut their eyes to avoid seeing what happened to them in the past,' he said. 'I, too, have started to remember what it was like in Santiago during the military coup. I remember the terror. Javier's death. And the rapes, Nana, right there at home, in our kitchen.'

Mira felt she could not draw breath. 'I don't want to,' she screamed.

But it was no longer possible to stop the images. The excited soldiers pushing each other in the queue leading to the girl, who was lying on the kitchen floor.

'No, no – I don't want to.'

'You have to.'

She saw that he was right, but still she shouted, 'You're wrong.'

Of course he was wrong, she told herself after he had left. He had said he'd be back the next day with a doctor.

'I've just got a cold.'

'You need something to help you sleep.'

Once more she paced through her flat, but she could no longer appeal to God. She knew what he would say. It was in the Bible: 'The Truth shall set you free.'

Mira never had seen the point of this.

When the phone rang, she checked the time. Only nine o'clock. What day? She wasn't sure.

She lifted the receiver, held it with both hands. It was Inge telling her about a lunch with a lawyer, who'd promised there would be an investigation. 'But, Mira, it might take a long time, it's all so complicated.'

'I see,' Mira said, getting the right words out sluggishly.

'Your voice sounds strange.'

'I've got a cold.'

'I'll phone again as soon as I find out anything else.'

'Right you are. Goodnight.'

Then Mira crawled back into bed and thought of how that London investigation was bound to be useless. That it was just another example of the usual Swedish insistence on managing the unknowable. Start an investigation, a commission of inquiry, that's what they always said in the radio news.

They try to deny fate, she thought. And when it deals a blow, they still like to think they can control it, these superior Swedes. Inge's the worst.

But at that moment God spoke to her in earnest. 'Inge is kind and wants to help you,' He said. 'Mira, you are unfair and ungrateful.'

She felt guilty and asked God to forgive her.

After that she slept.

CHAPTER 16

The Larraino family had gathered in the drawing room before dinner, as they did every day. Glasses of dry sherry were drunk while they discussed any news.

The inquiry was chaired by the head of the family, Fernando Larraino. He was a tall, silver-haired man, who had so distanced himself from ordinary life that he seemed surrounded by a vacuum.

His grandson bore his name, but was called Nano. No one would have dreamed of adding an affectionate twist to

Señor Fernando's name. Matilde did not address him as Daddy but as Father, and Nano called him Grandfather.

'So,' he said, turning to Nano, 'what is she like, this potential mother-in-law of yours?'

Nano hesitated. 'She is a tall blonde. Good-looking. Her movements are slow and somehow dignified.'

The old man raised his eyebrows and Nano realised that what he had said was not good enough. 'She's very direct.'

Fernando Larraino sighed discreetly and turned to Matilde. 'Nano has described her well,' she said. 'She does move slowly, in striking contrast with the speed of her mind. She's a cultured, reserved person, with the knack of making you confide in her – talk too much, maybe. A truthful woman.'

Fernando Larraino looked displeased. 'You know that I find these straight-from-the-shoulder, rather self-righteous people hard going. They usually cause trouble.'

'You've got the wrong idea,' Matilde said. 'If there's one thing about Inge Bertilsson I'm certain of, it's that she has a sense of humour.'

The old man shook his head. Humour was something he had difficulty understanding and consequently distrusted.

When they went in to dinner, Nano muttered to his mother that they'd presented a false picture of Inge Bertilsson. Matilde whispered back that the old boy had had his version in place from the start and that whatever they'd said would only have confirmed what he already knew.

Back at the guest-house, Inge and her daughters were drinking beer and making sandwiches. The conversation was not unlike that in the Chelsea drawing room.

'What did you think of Matilde, Mummy?'

'I liked her a lot.'

'But she's so awfully beautiful,' Ingrid said.

'I know, it's hard to take, isn't it? But we've got to put up with it.'

They all laughed.

'I can tell you now why it was so important for me to meet her.' And Inge told them about Mira's daughter, who had disappeared.

Ingrid and Britta listened in silence. Inge made it clear that they must not tell anyone about it.

'How did you know that Matilde . . . ?'

'Nano told me. He said she had connections that reached into the centre of the underground movement in Chile. She has often worked on problems connected with disappearances.'

'I had no idea,' Ingrid said.

'I knew that. Nano told me,' Britta said, beaming.

'Hey, boasted, more like,' Ingrid said. 'He must have known it would make a good impression.'

Britta blushed.

A few evenings later the Bertilsson family were invited for dinner with Señor Fernando Larraino. Britta was terrified, Ingrid tense and Inge calm. Maybe a little too calm, she thought, as they joined the family for sherry in the drawing room.

The room was decorated as if to form a backdrop for the ceremonies of a distant past. The chairs were almost painfully uncomfortable.

Nano and Britta preferred to stand. She had laid a proprietary hand on his shoulder.

After a slow start, the conversation rumbled along easily enough. Fernando asked all the usual questions about Sweden and Inge gave all the usual answers: large area, vast natural resources, small homogeneous population. And, of course, the long period of peace.

He seemed only moderately interested. His next question concerned the tactics of carrying out a socialist revolution without bloodletting. Her eyebrows raised, Inge replied rather sharply that there had been no revolution in Sweden.

'But surely you have a socialist government?'

'So do the British. And it's elected in the same way as our Swedish government.'

By now, there was a slight tension in the air. Inge caught Matilde's eye and she winked back. The corners of her mouth seemed to twitch with a repressed smile. So Inge continued, 'I suppose your question really concerns the means by which the Swedes achieved a strong, democratic working–class movement so early and so peacefully?'

'Well, you could put it that way.'

Inge smiled her sunniest smile. 'I have worked out an answer of my own to that question, but please remember that I'm a teacher and likely to be biased. Sweden was the first country in the world to legislate for compulsory public schooling. From 1842 onwards all children have learnt to read.' She paused and added as an afterthought, 'That reform was completed by an old-fashioned stable state, where social inequality was seen as God-given.'

'I don't think I quite see the point you're making.' He sounded interested.

'I believe it was literacy that gave rise slowly to political awareness of social injustice.'

'In other words, you're arguing that once the lower classes reach a certain level of education, the socialists will start winning elections?'

'It seems self-evident to me. After all, so far the working classes have made up the majority everywhere.'

'You've confirmed one of my fundamental views. There's no point in educating the lower classes. They don't actually need it and the only certainty is dangerous social unrest.'

Inge tried to hide her surprise and looked around the drawing room, reflecting that she had been right to feel that this was a place where time had stood still.

She said nothing more. But Señor Fernando wanted to continue the conversation and became confrontational: 'My grandson will inherit from me. He wants to marry your daughter. What do you make of that?'

Inge's voice was many degrees cooler when she said, 'I have no right in that regard. My daughter is a grown woman and makes her own decisions.'

'Your answer tells me that you're reneging on your parental responsibility.'

'I think it shows my respect for my daughter as an adult, who must make choices of her own.'

Matilde laughed at this, but she sounded sad when she said, 'Father has had certain bitter experiences of that.'

He seemed unmoved and did not look at Matilde. Instead he addressed Inge once more: 'And what if these two young people in love make a mistake?'

'It's their right,' Inge said, and added, remembering her own life, 'It is true – and here we agree, Señor – that they will have to pay a high price.'

A little later they went in to dine and Inge realised, amazed, that she had been subjected to an inquisition. Their host continued, after the soup had been cleared away: 'I think your daughter must be a strong-minded woman. My grandson will have a wife he cannot rule.'

'I do hope so,' Inge said, emphatically.

This time Matilde did not hold back her laughter, Ingrid

joined in and Nano smiled a little. Inge, too, looked amused as she went on: 'Britta is perfectly capable of earning an income of her own, so I don't need to ask Nano if he is able to support a wife. I might demand to be told if they were going to be nice to each other. But there's no way they could give me a truthful answer, because they do not yet know how unpredictable marriage can be.'

'It's all very simple,' Nano said. 'We love each other.'

Inge turned to the young man, and her smile was tender now. 'But, with a little effort, surely you can see that, briefly leaving love aside, there are all kinds of complications. Britta is poor, she belongs to a different social class and has been formed by a culture in which equality between the sexes amounts to something like religious conviction.'

'These things don't seem problematic to me,' Nano said. 'My problems lie here.'

The first few seconds of silence dragged on to become minutes. Then Nano pulled himself together and said, as if nothing untoward had happened, 'I want blond children with blue eyes.'

'Haven't you thought of the possibility that your children might have black eyes and high Indian cheekbones, like yours?' Inge asked.

He smiled. 'No, I haven't,' he said. 'It doesn't actually matter.'

'I promise you, you'll love a little Indian lad, darker than yourself.'

Britta said that maybe after that they'd have a blue-eyed Viking girl.

'So what?' Inge said, and thought that love can make clever women sound like silly little girls.

Afterwards they drank coffee in the drawing room. Señor

Fernando suddenly looked old and tired. He thanked them all for an interesting evening, and Inge said how much they had enjoyed the excellent meal. When he had withdrawn, Ingrid said to Matilde, 'Tell us, what is this family drama we seem to have joined for the evening?'

'Don't ask. The explanation would take all night.'

'And we're all very tired,' Inge said.

CHAPTER 17

Mira had been given sleeping tablets. She had slept off her fear, but when she woke she found herself in the grip of despair, which was almost worse.

Her cough was better now, though, so she could go back to work. Her first job at the nursery had been as the cook, but the staff soon realised that she was good with children. Also, she was the only one who could calm the Chileans when they felt anger or sadness of a kind that could only be expressed in Spanish.

Eduardo, who was four years old, spotted Mira when she arrived. His outrage at her recent abandonment took him over to such an extent that she had to sit on a stool in the hall and let him hit her. The small fists hammered against her and she felt pleased that she was wearing a thick coat.

'Where've you been?' he shouted in Spanish.

'I've been ill in bed in my house.'

He kept on hitting her. 'My mummy is ill too but she's got to work all the same. It's not fair.'

Mira grasped the furious hands in a firm grip, looked straight into the child's eyes and said to him that if you work in a day-nursery you mustn't come in when you're ill because the children might catch your illness. His mummy worked in a factory and the machines couldn't catch a cold.

He relaxed, climbed up into her lap and cried, but not for long. Soon he ran off outside to play with the other children.

'You're so good with them. How did you get round him?' the senior teacher, Lisbeth, asked her. Lisbeth was very competent but driven by ambition. Mira explained and Lisbeth sighed – she should have known, she said.

'Why should you?'

Lisbeth hesitated momentarily, then said, 'Don't get me wrong, but there's something strange about the Latin children. Joy or grief, they go completely over the top.'

'Aha, I see what you mean,' Mira said. 'They haven't been bent into shape yet.'

'You mean "haven't adjusted", don't you?'

Mira nodded and went into the kitchen, thinking that maybe that was the problem with Chile: nobody ever adjusted.

She started cooking and let the immigrant children come in to help with shaping the meatballs. She felt free to close the kitchen door while they chatted together in Spanish. When Lisbeth looked in, Mira said that the children needed their own language just now.

And it did me some good too, she thought, as she walked home. Spring was all around her, and the park and the old trees along the street glowed and smelt sweet. But when she unlocked her front door, the gnawing sensation inside her chest returned. She stretched out on her bed and told herself that the misery inside her came because she had lost her anger. Maybe it was anger that had kept her going during all the lonely years in Sweden. 'Without anger, despair can get to you,' she said aloud.

She wanted to start up a conversation with God.

But He did not listen.

He, too, has abandoned me, she thought.

For a while she felt tempted to take all the magic pills and disappear. Then she remembered that both her sons were coming for supper. She had to get up and go shopping. She would get some fish, expensive white-fleshed cod, which both Nesto and José liked. And fresh rhubarb. Pudding would be a pie with home-made custard.

I'll survive, she said to herself, when she was cooking. Despair had crawled up inside her and grabbed her by the throat. Breathe deeply, regularly. But she could only pant.

That was when she recalled the bottle, the gift that was to be kept for emergencies and had been put away in the cupboard with the nice china. She had never quite seen the point of the Swedish expression about emergencies. Now she understood: this was what it had come to.

It might help, she thought. At least, it won't kill you.

She forced the burning fluid down her gullet, in short, determined gulps. Then the phone rang. It was Nesto, who said that Gabriel had just returned from a trip to Chile and had many stories to tell. Surely she had cooked enough for him too.

She wanted to shout at him, in her usual way, but of course her anger had left her. Actually, all her faculties seemed adrift. Her head was singing and the kitchen floor was moving up and down like waves at sea.

She giggled. 'Goodness, I'm drunk,' she said, and tried to feel ashamed of herself. But she could not, because the ache in the pit of her stomach had vanished.

78

'Now I know how people become alcoholics.' She spoke aloud and, in a dizzying moment, thought she heard God laugh.

Maybe He had not abandoned her after all.

Then she scolded herself. The laughter had to be a fantasy caused by her being drunk out of her mind.

'Being drunk out of one's mind' was another one of these slightly puzzling Swedish expressions. Now, she knew exactly what it meant. 'Bloody hell,' she said. 'Must sober up.'

Nesto used to say that coffee helped, so she made herself a cup. It seemed to work as the floor settled down a little. When the boys arrived, she was upright and in full control, although she tried to avoid speaking.

Mira had always liked Gabriel, who was another Chilean. He was a short, chubby man. Normally irrepressibly good-humoured, he now seemed subdued and saddened.

'My mother's dead,' he said. 'But I got home in time to be with her.'

The men ate heartily and praised her cooking. All is almost normal, Mira thought. But she remained sitting while José cleared the table and Nesto wiped it clean.

Gabriel had brought a large map of Santiago and a pile of postcards. He spread out his map and pointed with a pencil. 'Here. I sneaked along one of these narrow lanes. Then I went via Calle del Puente to the Plaza de Armas. It looked just as grand as I remembered. It was the way it always was, with the towering cathedral and the crowds in the plaza. Remember, there'd be the chaps who offered to draw people's portraits, and photographers with ancient cameras and youths playing guitar. And transvestites all over

79

the place. They were all there still, as if nothing had happened.' His voice recalled his surprise.

He spread out his postcards, but Mira felt that she had no need to look. She saw it in her mind's eye, as it had been and as it still was, if Gabriel was to be believed.

He went on, 'Suddenly a loudspeaker started blasting out a song. It was Violeta Parras singing "Gracias A La Vida". You've heard it here, there's a Finnish woman who sings it in Swedish: "I Want To Thank Life".'

They hummed and sang it uncertainly, mixing Spanish and Swedish.

José asked, 'Are you telling us nothing had changed?'

'Well, yes, it has, it looks better, things are nicely done. Flowers, lots of them, planted along the streets and in the squares. Terrific advertising posters everywhere and all the young people are dressed like North American students.'

'So it's wealthier?'

'That's what I thought at first. Then I noticed the beggars. I'm not sure, but there did seem to be more of them than before. I could hardly look at the children with their hands stretched out and their hungry eyes, but then, I suppose, that might have to do with Sweden and being unused to it.'

They all understood what he meant. Gabriel went on, 'The police were different. Now there are many more of them and they seem better organised. And they're scared. They've got every reason to be. Apparently one of the mobile police-posts on the Plaza de Armas was blown up.'

Gabriel sat quietly for a while, then said: 'The Moneda Palace has been restored – it looks really smart. It made me feel so odd. In September 1973, when I saw it last, it was in flames.'

He pulled out the new cards showing the presidential

palace, but Mira had caught a glimpse of a view over the city with the white peak of the Aconcagua volcano in the background. She longed to be at home. The ache inside her had returned.

Gabriel started to describe how he went home to Carrascal by bus. 'You see, Pinochet had walls built round some of the *poblaciónes*.'

Mira had heard of these walls and tried to imagine what they would look like. Afterwards she had thought that the endless suburbs of Santiago had always been surrounded by walls, invisible but solid.

Gabriel said that the reason for building these walls was that the police did not dare confront the wild poor of the *poblaciónes*. For a moment, Mira felt proud of her people. But then he added that it could well be that the walls were there so that the tourists should not have to see the slums.

'It was very painful to arrive at my mother's house. *Dios*, the misery of it, dirty and patched. Hopeless. When I was a child I liked it. Over the years I've even been thinking in a foolish, romantic way about the lanes back home. But then I stood there watching my sisters and my sisters' many children, all of them dirty and hungry and wearing greyish rags, washed with cheap soap in cold water. It had not occurred to me to bring food with me, only stupid gifts. I felt like a kicked dog. There I was in my fine clothes. I was homesick too and that didn't help. I wanted to get back to Sweden, to my own kitchen and my own bathroom. I wanted to see my neighbours, cool Swedes who'd never talk and shout all at the same time and who'd never push me up against a wall and ask prying questions. There, our house was crowded with relatives and neighbours. I was being cross-examined. They wanted to know everything, most of all about me and women.'

Mira was no longer listening. She was tired and wished that they would all go away. José, who noticed such things, told her to go to bed.

She fell asleep, heavy-headed from the brandy. The images of Santiago were fluttering behind her closed eyelids. She woke in the middle of the night. The ache in the pit of her stomach had lessened, still gnawing but unpleasantly rather than unbearably. Then she realised that she had a headache painful enough to distract her from the pain in her chest.

She sat up: something seemed to be thumping inside her forehead and there were flashing lights before her eyes.

She tried once more to find the Swedish words – there were plenty when it came to drinking alcohol. She found the right one and smiled with relief: she wasn't ill, she had a hangover. And a splitting headache.

Time for coffee and aspirins, she said to herself.

She went slowly along to the kitchen. The blessed lads, they'd done the dishes.

After a while the banging and thumping seemed to die down enough to let her think.

Gabriel had said something important in passing. What was it?

It came back to her. He had mentioned being especially scared during the earthquakes, because he had forgotten what they were like.

Me too, she said to herself. I had even forgotten the relief I felt when I arrived in this country and was told there were no earthquakes in Sweden.

Then, all at once, she remembered Valparaiso and how people there could practically set their clocks by the 'quakes. She recalled how she and her father had sat, high up on the cliffs, looking at the lifts, the famous seventeen

82

lifts, going up and down the rock-faces. Below, surrounded by the unending sea, was an island called Isla Negra and on it stood Neruda's house. Sitting on her father's lap, she listened while he read to her from a book of Neruda's poems and waited for the 'quake. It came punctually, to the minute.

My father, she thought. I loved him. The wound near my heart opened when he left me for ever.

CHAPTER 18

When she was walking to work the next morning Mira took the longer way round: fresh air was what she needed. She could not get over her forgetfulness: how could she have failed to remember the earthquakes?

She wondered how to put it to Lisbeth at the nursery. You see, she would say, people who live with death lurking under the ground find it hard to adjust to a long, carefully planned life.

Then she snorted.

Never would she be able to talk to a Swede of the fear that drove people out of their houses at night, some still in their nightwear, others with coats slung over their shoulders, all with children in their arms, and the older children carrying little ones. She could hear it now, the sound of bare feet running over the shaking ground. And she could remember the laughter when it was all over and they were walking back to their houses. Laughing at old Juan, who had emerged naked and ghostly white from his house, and at the mother who had been carrying her child by the feet, head down. *Dios mio*, how that child had howled.

The hysterical sense of relief somehow demanded togetherness, silly stories and lots of laughter.

The young children coped with it best: they just fell asleep in the women's laps. The street dogs behaved in the same way: they curled up in the roadside dust and slept as if nothing had happened. But it was always their shrill barking that woke people when the ground under their homes started to tremble.

She could remember when a big earthquake had wrecked the cities in Chile's southern regions. She had been a little girl then, held in her father's arms, sheltering with him under the arched gateway leading into the street. He said that it was properly built, with stone and mortar according to Roman principles, and would resist even the worst of the shocks. Tall, handsome buildings collapsed in the centre of Santiago. The suburbs got away with it more lightly.

Almost eight o'clock – she had to get to work.

Once she was at the nursery, there was much to occupy her. A little Chilean girl had a sore tummy and Mira, the only one who could talk to her, had to accompany her to see a doctor. She cried so much in the health centre that the staff let her in ahead of the other patients. There is something to be said for the Chilean temperament, Mira thought.

The doctor examined the girl meticulously, but could not find anything wrong. 'It might be anxiety that's upset her,' he said. Mira remembered that the child's parents were divorcing. She told the doctor, who looked sad and prescribed a tranquilliser. The little girl slept in the tram on the way back, while Mira was thinking of how almost all

Chilean married couples divorced after arriving in Sweden. She had done exactly that and knew why.

God help her, she had been so happy when the Swedish authorities had put her husband on the plane to Argentina, and handed her the divorce papers. And on the day she had opened a bank account in her own name and paid in money she had earned herself. A bank account in her own name: it was unbelievable. Her feet had tapped swiftly along the pavements on her way home, as if she'd been dancing.

I must tell Inge about this, she thought.

That day after work she did not feel like going home to the flat. She did not want to give in to the brandy and the pills. Instead she found herself walking to the new estate and soon she was facing Inge's garden and terraced house. She saw that the weeds were taking over, both in the borders and on the slope towards the cliffs.

Now she knew what to do.

First, she had to call on Kerstin, the neighbour, who had the key. They had met once at Inge's over a cup of coffee and afterwards Inge had said that the woman's heart was in the right place. Mira had realised long ago that the Swedes used this phrase about all kinds of people – even drunkards or fools. Mira had become quite clear recently about where her own heart was located. It was in the pit of her stomach, deep inside her ribcage where it swung upwards in the midline.

The neighbour seemed pleased to see Mira – the weeds in Inge's garden had worried her too. And there was a growing pile of letters and faxes from the publishers.

'Couldn't you have phoned her?'

'I don't know her number.'

But Mira did, because she had a photographic memory for numbers. She rattled off the long sequence.

'Maybe you'd better phone, Mira,' said Kerstin.

Of course Mira would phone, no problem, but she needed the key. She also wanted to get into the house to find an overall and a pair of boots.

Inside the air was stale, so she opened all the windows and doors. Then she thought she might as well tidy up. Inge wouldn't be offended – she probably wouldn't even notice.

As the draughts whistled through the house, Mira read the last fax from Inge's publishers. They had sold the rights in the book somewhere abroad, and since the foreign firm needed to translate it, could Inge please hurry up?

There were many more of the same kind, all ending 'Keep in touch.'

Mira was pleased to find the impatient faxes: they might prompt Inge to come home straight away. She dialled the number, but there was no reply. I'll try again a little later, she thought.

She equipped herself with a trowel, a rake and a short, sharp knife, and got started at the top of the rocky slope. As she worked, she could feel some of the old anger welling up. 'Effing thing,' she said to every dandelion. And when she confronted the creeping buttercup and its long snarled-up stems, her eyes narrowed: 'Don't think you're going to get the better of me by tying yourself in knots.'

After a couple of hours her back was hurting, but that was all right, and the pit of her stomach was complaining. She stretched, washed her hands in the kitchen and tried telephoning again.

Inge answered at once: 'Where have you been? We've been trying to reach you all afternoon.'

Mira's heart was thumping painfully. 'Any news?'

'Perhaps. You'd better talk to the lawyer.'

A cultured Chilean voice started speaking. Mira recognised the upper-class accent and tried not to feel irritated. She found something to sit on just in time.

'The officials have informed me that the woman named Otilia Narvaes died after a short stay in a detention camp for women.'

'It cannot be true. She would have come to me in the night.'

'I believe you,' said the lovely voice. 'It is always easier for the authorities to enter 'Deceased' in response to applications for information.'

There was a pause. Mira could think of nothing to say. Then the voice continued, 'One of our . . . contacts knows a woman a few years older than your daughter. It seems they were in the detention camp at the same time. She escaped, married and is now living in England. We'll try to get in touch with her.'

'Thank you,' Mira said. 'Thank you a thousand times.'

The lawyer continued, 'You wouldn't have a picture of your daughter?'

'No, but I have one of my mother. They were very alike.'

'I'll talk to you again when we've found the other woman I mentioned.'

They said *buenas tardes* to each other and the call was at an end.

Mira was on her way home when she realised that she had not mentioned the faxes to Inge. I'll call her tomorrow, she said to herself.

Then she remembered that the lawyer had referred to

87

Otilia as 'the woman'. Slowly it dawned on Mira that her daughter would be an adult now.

What would she look like?

This was when Mira invented the daydreams that made her life easier. The longest and nicest was about how Otilia had managed to jump out of the armoured car and crawl on all fours into a doorway. A Dutchman had found her there and brought her to his embassy. When she had been nursed back to her old self, he had fallen in love with her. They had married and left together. Now she was the wife of a Dutch market gardener. Mira could picture her strolling along the paths between huge fields of tulips, like the ones in a photo Mira had cut out of a magazine and stuck up on the kitchen wall. Otilia walked along with the gardener. He was older than her, which Mira thought was a good thing.

When Mira was in her flat the images kept coming. Otilia was sitting on a bench in front her house, a long, low, solid building, like a Swedish farmhouse. There were two children playing at her feet, a boy and a girl . . .

Mira found it difficult to visualise the children's faces, which was frustrating because she wanted to see who in the family they were most like.

She went on watching her images in bed, aware that this was just a game, or all damned lies, as the Swedes put it.

She took her sleeping pills and still felt heavy-headed when she phoned Inge the next morning to tell her about the faxes.

Inge sounded pleased. She said she missed home and had done what she had had to do in London. She'd get a flight to Arlanda as soon as possible.

Later that morning, Inge called the nursery to say that she would arrive at one o'clock on Saturday. Mira approved of that: it would give her time to finish weeding the garden and tidying the house.

CHAPTER 19

Of course, they said all the right things to each other when they parted at Heathrow: Ingrid said she was sorry Inge had to leave, Britta said she had hoped they would have more time to talk, and Inge said she really didn't want to go but had to finish her book – the foreign contract would bring in quite a lot of money. But she was smiling when she passed through passport control – none of them had been truthful. All three were secretly pleased her visit was over: Britta because the man she loved was no longer under her mother's scrutiny, Ingrid because she was now free to have a go at her sister, who had obviously lost her head, and Inge because she just longed to get home.

She used to love London, but this time she had seen what Matilde had observed: the underbelly of the city – the lowest layer of the class structure, where the prostitutes and homeless existed, and where the thousands of immigrants fought for survival.

In the aeroplane, Inge heard in her mind fragments of conversation from the last few days. This surprised her a little. Had her memory improved?

First Matilde: 'I've got a man, but not the relationship you might have imagined. He's intelligent and witty, and he cares for me.' She smiled and continued: 'He has a most unusual talent for friendship. And he's homosexual, which means that I can keep some things to myself, if you see what I mean.'

'Yes, I do. I, too, had a male friend rather like yours. And, like you, I felt I could be honest when I was with him. I was not expected to play games.'

She had paused to remember what it had been like. 'He helped me through the bad years. It started with him babysitting when I had to work in the evenings. The kids loved him – he took them skiing or into town to the cinema or the theatre. He read them stories – he was an academic and literature was his subject so he knew what to tell and how.' There was a lump in her throat as she said, 'He was always there. He listened patiently to my weeping and wailing, the whole sad story of how unfairly life had treated me. I told everyone else I was fine, happy, well and enjoying my new freedom.'

'Did you lose touch?'

Inge closed her eyes – her whole face seemed to close. 'He died. He had Aids.'

For a while they sat in silence. Matilde broke it: 'We seem to understand each other very well, you and I.'

'No, I don't think so. Ever since we talked in that taxi, I've been trying to understand what it did to you, the torture and . . . being raped. I think I would have died. Matilde, you're much stronger than I.'

'I'm not so sure. You see, I wasn't allowed to die, they saw to that. They put me on drips, gave me drugs, injections.'

'Dear God, why?'

'They arrested me to get me to tell them where my lover was. The hiding-place he and his guerrilla fighters used. I would have betrayed him, Inge – you must understand this, I would have said anything and everything. But I knew nothing, Pedro had taken care of that. I have no memory of when they let me go. It was only later that I was told they threw me out into the street because they had shot Pedro. I have glimpses of when I stayed in the British embassy where civilised people, doctors, looked after me. But the ambassador kept a dog ... Anyway, they flew me to London and a hospital bed was found for me immediately. My son was four. Imagine what it was like for him. When his grandmother took him to hospital to see me, there was just this ghostly white parcel, with tubes poking into it surrounded by gurgling machines. Bandages covered my face. You see, they had to operate on it. The dogs ... Well, there were scars. There are some excellent plastic surgeons in England.'

Inge groaned. She remembered that she had assumed Matilde's smooth skin was a sign that life had treated her gently.

'You ask how I can live with memories like that. The past is dispatched into the shadows – but it can trick you and come back, maybe at night or during the day, called up by some casual remark. Then the ground opens and you fall into an abyss of fear. It was that friend of mine, the man I mentioned, who made me see that I had to get into that hell, remember everything and tell my friends about it. After that, I could work with others who had endured the same things. You'll understand that, the strange comfort you get from knowing that you're not alone in facing ... things that cannot be understood.

'As far as Nano was concerned, I was never his real mother.' For a moment, Matilde seemed about to break down, but she continued. 'His mother was his grand-mother, a woman with firm views on how to bring up boys. But she, too, abandoned him: she died, slowly, from cancer. The only person left to care for the boy was his grandfather and he lives in a Never-never Land of the past. His only goal for Nano was that he should become an English gentleman.'

Inge could not remember how she and Matilde had parted that afternoon. But she hadn't forgotten the conversation with Britta. They had sat on Inge's bed until late at night. The house was cold, so they wrapped themselves in the spare blankets. Britta was sane and sensible. And very angry.

'I know what you're thinking. You think Nano is a nobody, someone without any will or identity of his own. But you know nothing about how life's treated him.'

'Yes, I do, Matilde's told me.'

'Has she? How odd. I didn't think she would dare admit . . .'

Inge said nothing.

'Is she sorry she abandoned him, then?'

'I didn't ask her that. But there's this thing about great love, which I don't understand but you seem to.'

They laughed together at this.

'Oh, Mummy, you're not as sensible as you think you are.'

'Well, OK, use me as an example. I was just as certain as you are now that I'd found the great love of my life.'

'And so you had. You never married again. Not Lars, for instance, who was such a nice man.' She looked quizzically at Inge then went on: 'Just remember what you feel about Daddy, how you said that you still love him.'

'On the whole I recovered quite quickly.'

'Are you sure?'

'No.'

'You know, Mother, your problem's that you never let yourself feel sorry for yourself.

'I know it's going to be easier for me and Nano.' Britta's voice was harsh. 'I'm so furious with that boarding-school. I'm sure you know more than I about what they really do to children in those exclusive English schools. Nano put up with it. He was fighting for some kind of identity. He would become an Englishman. It took time for him to realise it was impossible. His accent was all right, but not his hair and his skin. Do you understand?'

'Yes, I do,' Inge said, and thought of Mira.

But she also thought of what her daughters had inherited from her: the ability to empathise with others and the need to care for them. She had fought this almost daily – her cool manner had developed from it.

She was surprised when they started preparing to land at Arlanda and pleased as they lost height over the tracts of cold-looking forest.

I'll take a taxi home from the airport, she thought.

But as soon as she was through Customs she saw Nesto, smiling broadly and waving to catch her attention. She knew at once that this was what she had hoped would happen, and the reason she had told Mira the time of her arrival.

'Goodness, this is so kind of you,' she said, as she gave him a hug. 'The idea of sitting on all those buses to get home was awful.'

'I've brought you a little surprise,' he said. 'Come and see.'

And there it was, a small Japanese car, strawberry-red and shiny, as if new.

'You don't have to buy it, of course,' he said. 'José found

93

it – it's a real bargain. Only ten thousand kronor. We've checked it out and fixed a few things. It's pretty well perfect now.'

Inge stood there in silence.

'It's easy enough to sell. Just tell us if you don't want it,' Nesto said. He had misunderstood her silence.

'Of course I want it.'

'Thought so,' Nesto said, and smiled. He put her suitcase into the boot and handed her the keys. 'It's an automatic.'

'So, there's no clutch?'

'That's right.'

For the first couple of miles Inge's left leg twitched, and her right hand kept reaching for the gear-lever. Then she got used to the car and began to enjoy the drive. It was quite a fast run. More than once Nesto had to say, 'Hey, watch your speed.'

When they neared Inge's house, he said, 'Inge, there's something wrong with Mother. She's not herself – she seems defeated somehow. She takes too many tablets and sometimes she gets a bit pissed.'

Silence. The car went more slowly.

'Maybe I picked up something like that from her voice,' Inge said. 'It seemed rather weak and toneless.'

'Yes, that fits in with everything else about her.'

'Is she waiting for me at the house?'

'No.'

'I'll ring her.'

'Good. I've got to get on right away.'

Nesto's minibus was parked outside Inge's house. He stepped into it and drove off at once.

'Got to collect more folk at Arlanda,' he said. 'This time it's just tourists.'

94

CHAPTER 20

Inge walked through her garden. Someone had been at work in it. It looked very pretty. Miniature narcissi were in flower on the rocky slope at the back of the house. There were pearl hyacinths and her wonderful white double anemones, looking like tiny white roses. But she was not happy. Not even the birdsong and the scent of the flowers gave her the pleasure she might have expected.

There was a tidy pile of faxes next to the telephone. She contacted her editor to say she was home and hoped to finish the book within a fortnight.

She could almost hear her heart beating when she dialled Mira's number.

'Hi, it's me. I've just got back.'

'Welcome home,' a frail voice replied.

'Nesto came to meet me. He brought the new car. Have you seen it?'

'No.'

'Listen, I thought I'd take it out for a run, maybe to the lakes. You know where I mean. Do you want to come too?'

Silence. Inge imagined what Mira would have said in the old days: 'Fantastic. I'll make a picnic.' This time she said, 'I suppose so.'

'I'll come and pick you up in half an hour.'

She was waiting outside the door to the block of flats. Like her voice, her body seemed to have shrunk, lost colour and dynamism.

Inge got out of the car and gave Mira a hug. It did not seem to bring them any closer. The thin body inside Mira's coat felt rigid, stick-like.

'First of all, I've got to thank you for looking after the garden.'

Mira nodded. 'I tidied up in the house as well.'

'Oh dear, I didn't notice.'

'I didn't expect you to.'

What can I do about her? Inge wondered, as she got into first gear and released the clutch – using the accelerator. The car shrieked. Mira laughed for the first time and said, 'At this rate you'll soon have it in pieces.'

They sat watching the lovely lake in silence, until Inge in desperation started describing the Larraino family. She called the batty old señor 'a dinosaur'.

'That type is pretty common in Chile,' Mira said. 'We call them mummies.'

'But his daughter is something else – just wait till I tell you about our lawyer.'

After listening a while, Mira said, 'You sound as if you were practically in love with her.' The voice was more like its old angry self. Inge did not dare smile, and went on telling the story of Matilde's love, how she met the young revolutionary, had a child with him then had to abandon it.

'I cannot understand women like that,' Mira said contemptuously.

They did not speak during the drive back to town. The old trust between them had gone, and both women missed it.

When they got closer to her home, Mira tried, 'I thought I'd tell you about my bank account.'

'Is there a problem with the bank?'

Mira shook her head. Her story didn't matter anyway.

Still, when they said goodbye, she added, 'I'll come tomorrow and set to work in the greenhouse. The plants need to get outside.'

'You're right, they need the wind and the sun,' Inge said, and tried to sound happy.

They were both lying, and both knew it.

CHAPTER 21

Inge woke that night and found she was crying. Afterwards she managed to get back to sleep.

In the morning she told herself to cheer up. Life must go on. She made coffee. Mira had thought of her and stocked up with bread, butter, cheese and marmalade.

She went through her mail and found bills, a couple of invitations to fiftieth-birthday celebrations, a letter from an old friend and a postcard from the West Indies. Someone who wants to boast about their holiday, she thought, turned the card over and immediately recognised the writing.

Jan!

This is crazy, she thought, as she read the brief message again and again: 'Please don't worry about me, all is well. They're short of good computer scientists here.'

It annoyed her. Why should I worry about him? Conceited fool, she thought.

Then she remembered Marilyn, her two little boys and how their money had disappeared. She phoned London.

'Oh, Mummy!' Britta exclaimed. 'Where did it come from?'

'I can't read the stamp, but the picture shows one of these stupid paradise beaches.'

'You've got to send it on, Mummy. The police here must have it.'

Inge did not like the idea, but gritted her teeth and promised. 'It's Sunday,' she said. 'Even if I send it by special delivery it might take a couple of days.'

'Wait. We'll get in touch with Marilyn's brother and call you back.'

While Inge waited for the call, her head filled with conflicting thoughts. Some of the time she thought, I don't want to do this. Then she thought, I must.

After a while a calm English voice spoke to her. Could she fax through a copy of the card? And a translation of the text? At once?

'Yes.' She was given a fax number and an address and agreed to send the card itself by special delivery.

Then she sat thinking about what Matilde had said: 'You see, I would have betrayed him if . . .' But she, Inge, had not been subjected to torture.

She looked through her manuscript, making corrections as she went. She considered the way the text was divided into chapters and thought about the things she had left to say in the conclusion. It all seemed straightforward.

Mira arrived at eleven o'clock and they tried to smile at each other. On the way to the greenhouse, they were getting on almost as easily as ever. There were so many practical things to talk about: which plants went into which pots and where best to put them on the patio.

'Listen to the birdsong, isn't it nice?'

'Yes,' said Mira, and smiled rather tightly.

While Mira did the planting Inge worked at her desk. Later

she cooked a chicken from the freezer and some rice to go with it. They ate. Inge dared to ask, 'What was the matter with your bank account?'

'Leave it, you wouldn't understand.'

That evening Inge drove Mira home. At the house she said, 'Can I come up and see how your African lilies are getting on?'

'By all means.'

The flat looked tidy and the lilies were thriving, although still not showing any buds. 'They'll come,' Inge said.

'Would you like a brandy?'

'I can't, I'm driving – remember?'

At that moment Inge realised that Mira wanted to get rid of her. What in the name of God can I do about this? she thought, as she hurried down the stairs.

When Inge got back the phone rang. The polite Englishman was on the line again, saying that the police had not been able to read the place-name in the franking on the faxed copy of the card. Had she sent the original?

'Yes, this afternoon. By special delivery,' Inge said, trying to speak so clearly that she could not possibly be misunderstood.

When she had put down the receiver, she thought of Jan and his vulnerability, his anxiety. He had trusted her. Oh, hell. Traitor! She had betrayed him.

The rest of that evening she spent recalling what Jan was like. She remembered that if the children were ill he used to vanish and she would try to stay awake, lying on the folding bed in the girls' room. He'd come back in the small hours, after too much drinking and . . . No! Yes, he'd rape her.

This was how she dealt quite successfully, if only

temporarily, with her feelings of guilt. Then she could escape into sleep.

The weeks crept past. Inge was writing like someone obsessed. Now and then Mira would come round after work. They would exchange a few words about the weather. It was worth talking about: sunshine and warmth poured down over Scandinavia.

One Saturday in June Ingrid came home. For a few hours at least, everything was as it should have been. Ingrid brought a piece of good news: Britta had been offered a place at the medical school in Stockholm.

'Surely she won't —'

'Of course not, she's not completely mad. She's worked so hard for this, you know. Think of all the time she's put in getting that ghastly work experience in the English health service.'

'And what about Nano?'

'Ask her.'

Then Inge had to talk about Mira. 'She's withdrawn, lost all her liveliness, she's often cold and unpleasant,' she said.

'What do her sons think?'

'They can't reach her either. They're beside themselves with worry, just like me.'

That afternoon Nesto turned up. He stared at Ingrid and said, 'I thought people looking like you only existed in magazines.'

'Oh, come off it, don't do the "pretty Swedish girl" bit. I'm not impressed.'

'I might have guessed.'

Inge and Nesto went into the study to talk business. He had brought an invoice, complete with VAT. Inge smiled with relief – she could easily pay what they were asking. But she had to say, 'Why haven't you charged for the check-up on my old car?'

'You must let us give you that. Inge, let's talk about Mother instead. What are we to do about her?'

And then they just sat there, hardly daring to look at each other.

Ingrid and Inge sat up all night talking until there was nothing left to say. Emptied at last, Inge thought with relief, when she finally fell into bed.

Sleep, sleep.

She woke when the sun had already climbed high into the sky. She heard voices in the kitchen.

Mira, who knew perfectly well that she was being unfair and behaving badly, had worked out how to feel better about herself. She went to Inge's house and cooked delicious meals, did the washing and ironing, made coffee and put a cup on Inge's desk.

This Sunday morning she had brought bread dough, already prepared and left to rise in her own kitchen. Now Inge would wake to the smell of freshly baked bread.

She was just putting it into the oven when she caught a glimpse of someone coming down the stairs. It was an angel.

The bright creature came downstairs slowly, as if sleep-walking. She said, 'What a lovely smell.' She looked at Mira, walked straight up to her, gave her a hug and said, 'Oh, Mira, Mummy has been talking so much about you and your little girl.' She was crying, the tears were running down her cheeks, and she kissed Mira and held her tightly.

Mira was deeply affected. This was a young Inge who had something her mother did not – or did not dare to show.

Like a child, she smelt of sleep and soap, and some kind of flower-scented shampoo.

Mira freed herself and looked searchingly into the big blue eyes. This girl *was* like an angel, and she thought, You've got to watch your back with the angelic ones. Then she broke down, threw herself on a chair by the kitchen table and wept.

The angel kept her mouth shut, thank goodness. Instead she settled on the kitchen floor, laid her head on Mira's lap and wept with her.

There Inge found them both. She said, 'The whole house smells of burning.'

Ingrid and Mira thought the same thing: Typical Inge.

But Inge had opened the oven door and smoke poured into the kitchen. 'Out,' she said. 'Why don't you go to the rose-bower and carry on from where you were?'

She gets some things right, Ingrid thought, and tottered outside with her arm round Mira.

The bower was a perfect place to weep for what you have lost for ever.

Meanwhile, Inge made herself a cup of instant coffee, found a stale cinnamon bun in the fridge and went to her desk.

It was a strange day in the small house. People moved about stealthily. In the afternoon Matilde phoned from London. They had found the woman who had been in the same camp as Otilia. She had agreed to meet Señora Narvaes and her family the following week.

'Is that all?'

'Yes,' Matilde answered. 'She wants to be quite sure before . . .'

In silence, they came to the same hard conclusion. Inge was given the woman's name, address and a telephone number in a Scottish village.

'She married a sheep-farmer,' Matilde said.

CHAPTER 22

Mira was lying on Inge's bed. Her face was swollen from crying, but she felt at peace. 'I'm not really stupid and mean,' she said aloud.

At once gentle agreement was apparent in the room. At last, God was listening. She sat up in bed, clasped her hands in prayer and said, 'It was bad of me to try to bribe You.'

He concurred, but said that He knew human beings could not bear too much reality. She had to ponder this for a while before she understood. 'Not all at once, anyway,' she said.

It was time for her to mourn now, He said.

She thought of her son Javier, who had been murdered during the curfew. She had never allowed herself time to mourn him.

She conjured up the image of Otilia walking across Dutch tulip-fields. Then she snorted with contempt, loudly. This time she was sure she heard God laughing.

Far away, the telephone in Inge's study was ringing.

O Dios, she thought, it's Sunday. And nobody here has had anything to eat, not even breakfast.

Now she could laugh at this morning's burnt offering.

She went to the kitchen and found another frozen chicken. It would do. She could hear Inge speaking on the phone in English. Mira's heart beat faster with anxiety. But when Inge came through to the kitchen, she just asked, 'Where's Ingrid?'

'I think she's having a shower.'

Inge looked long and hard at Mira. Mira's eyes were bloodshot but her gaze was calm. Dear Lord, Inge thought, how can I tell her this?

They sat at the kitchen table and looked mutely at each other. Then Ingrid came downstairs wearing jeans and a white shirt. Her hair was wet and her eyelids swollen.

'My angel,' Inge said.

'Has she always been like this?' Mira asked. Inge nodded, and remembered how much she had worried about this sweet, generous child.

Then she pulled herself together and told Mira about the call from London. 'You see, Mrs Drummond refuses to speak to anyone except a member of Otilia's family,' Inge explained.

God was right, now it is time to mourn, Mira thought. 'Yes.'

'We've got to speak to your sons.'

'Would you please do that?' Mira begged.

'Of course.'

Inge got hold of Nesto, who was in a garage inspecting the undercarriage of his bus. He said he was to drive to Poland the next day. 'In that case you've got to come here tonight,' Inge said, in her sternest tone. He said OK, he'd be there, give or take an hour.

José, too, answered his mobile phone. Yes, no problem, except his wife was working the night-shift so he had to go home and pick up Lars-José. Would Inge call Kristina, and explain, please?

'Of course,' Inge said.

Inge had met Kristina and had recognised the type at once. This was the prettiest girl in the class, laughing eyes under long lashes, a smile playing at the corners of her mouth, and large breasts. She would laugh rather than giggle, and was talented enough, but uninterested in schoolwork.

She had liked those girls and often defended them in the school common room: they were prey to early hormonal tumult, she would argue. If they found the right man, they would be good wives and mothers.

She told Kristina about the call from England and the trip they had to make to Scotland the following week.

'But won't that mean she . . . ?'

'We've no idea. And, of course, she needs to be certain.'

'Tell José that he must go with Mira. I've got quite a lot of time off next week and, besides, my mother will help out. Don't worry, I'll manage.'

So they arrived, both Mira's sons. Nesto held his mother's hand while Inge told them about the phone call. They had to go.

There was quite a lot of debate about which day, but Inge cut it short: 'We've simply got to let Mrs Drummond decide.'

They nodded and Inge dialled. A boy's voice answered and she asked for Mrs Drummond. While she waited, she gave Mira the receiver and said that she had to speak, as the next of kin.

'I can't speak English.'

'But she'll speak Spanish, of course.'

'I want to go too,' Lars-José shouted, but was instantly

quiet when he heard the gravity in José's voice: 'No, you can't.'

'Tuesday seems all right,' Mira said, and put down the receiver. 'That day Eloiza is alone at home. But, Inge, none of us speaks English.'

Then the angel smiled and said that she'd come with them.

CHAPTER 23

Inge would be on her own for a few days. She was looking forward to this – she needed time alone. She had finished the manuscript and sent the text on computer disk to the publishers.

Her garden was in full flower and bathed in the light of early summer.

The evening before Ingrid left for England, mother and daughter had a farewell drink together. Ingrid was worried: 'Mummy, you look exhausted.'

'I'm worrying all the time about Mira. And about Jan. And Britta too.'

They were quiet for a time, gazing thoughtfully at the red wine in their glasses.

'I didn't know you were worrying about Britta. In London your attitude seemed so relaxed, maybe even mildly amused.'

This made Inge flush with annoyance and conversation stopped again. Then she said, using her usual technique of finding a route around an obstacle, 'It's hard to have grown-up children, you know. A mother is supposed to keep herself to herself and not to express any opinions. She's reduced to an ineffectual bystander, keeping a sympathetic mumsy smile permanently in place.'

Her voice was getting louder. Ingrid replied, 'Who laid down *that* law?'

'I did,' Inge said, and remembered her own mother, who had often warned her against Jan.

No one spoke for a while and through the silence came the notes of a blackbird's evening song.

'You never know, Mother, life for Britta and Nano may turn out better than we think.'

Inge did not answer but her face spoke volumes.

They raised their glasses and drank a toast to 'love'. They were sitting outside and though the clock told them it was evening, the sun was still up. Its rays raked through the garden where the trees, leaf-buds newly open, were whispering to each other. The sycamores were in bloom and the faint breeze smelled of honey.

'But why does Daddy worry you so much?' Ingrid asked.

'He doesn't. Not really. It's just that sometimes I feel like a traitor.'

'I don't understand. Anyway, you worry about Mira as well.'

'Yes, indeed.'

It was still light when they went to bed at midnight, but the colour of the sky had become a deeper blue. Next morning at five, José was due to collect Ingrid. Inge had taken a tablet to make sure she would get some sleep. The last thing she thought that evening was that now she'd have time to keep her diary.

She woke when the car arrived and ran downstairs in her dressing-gown. There was just time to hug Mira. Feeling

Mira's body go softer in response to the hug, Inge thought that she's got no idea . . .

Then she went back to bed and tried to go to sleep, but her thoughts hovered around Britta and Nano. What would happen when Britta returned to Sweden and went to medical school? Would her love be over then, like influenza? But surely it was just as likely that love would flourish and became a passion, sustained by distance and dreams. For passion seems to feed off impossible situations, like the loved one living in Australia or being married.

'He is no one,' Britta had admitted of Nano. But those who are no one in themselves can be wonderful mirrors for others.

Having got this far, Inge felt ashamed of herself. She knew nothing about Nano Larraino. And as for the great love of one's life, her own experience had been brief and sad.

At this point, her mind drifted to Jan. This would not do. Resolutely she got out of bed, went to the bathroom and ended up staring at herself in the mirror as she had done so many times before she had met Mira.

And as on those many times before, she asked herself if one could trust what one sees. Perhaps, she thought, one picks and chooses visual images to fit pre-established patterns. Adult eyes are never innocent, she told herself, closing her own, turning away from the mirror and brushing her teeth. She massaged cream into her skin and had begun to brush her hair, when she caught a glimpse of another, younger Inge behind the face in the mirror. Someone like Ingrid, not as beautiful, but pretty. This was how she had looked when she had fallen in love with Jan.

And now she could admit that the warning bells had been ringing much more strongly for herself than for Britta.

Nano was a boy, but he might grow into an adult. Jan had already been grown-up, a man with a strong will and set goals. He was not interested in love, only sex.

Was that the truth?

She put on a big comfortable shirt and a pair of old trousers. Making coffee in the kitchen, her mind constantly circled round the same questions.

That pretty twenty-five-year-old, who had she been?

Alone and starved of love. She had not belonged to those ready to enjoy the new sexual atmosphere of the time. I was a naïve dreamer, who had overdosed on romantic poetry, Inge thought. I believed love meant that two halves met to form a whole and individual goals and needs were shared.

Dear God, why had that girl forgotten all her earlier aspirations? She had decided to be free, never depend on anyone and never give up the right to shape her life on her own terms.

Of course, she had not really forgotten, and that was the beginning of the end.

Inge took her coffee and went to sit on a stone at the back of the garden and enjoy the sunshine. Heavy-bodied bumble-bees were humming among her white double anemones, the ones that looked like roses.

Matilde and Inge had talked about love of the kind that hits you like lightning from a clear sky and knocks all the sense out of you. They had been sitting in a London café with cups of tea. Matilde had insisted that falling in love was a kind of profound recognition. That person is the right one for me, he sees the world as I do, thinks my thoughts, feels my emotions and knows my secrets, even those I have refused to admit to myself.

She had gone on to say that such love is a miracle. You are no longer an outsider, but instead allowed to be who you are. You have nothing to hide any more and no need to be defensive.

Inge's first response had been silence. She felt both surprised and provoked. Finally she had said, rather crisply, that the whole thing sounded like a projection of self.

She remembered how Matilde had looked at her with pity, which Inge resented. She had to ask: 'How do you think your love would have turned out if you had married and lived together in normal circumstances for a long time?'

'I think both of us knew that Death was walking at our side, always. That certainty was there in Pedro's eyes and his hands and his immense tenderness.'

For once, Inge had not said what she thought, which was that joining Love and Death in that way sounded pretentious.

Now, sitting on the rock with her garden spread in front of her, she could admit that she had been envious.

Her thoughts were interrupted by Kerstin, her neighbour, who came round to ask if Inge would give Caesar his breakfast. Caesar was a large yellow tom-cat, given to prowling along the fences at the back of the terrace. Kerstin was about to go into town on an errand.

Inge liked the cat. He was old, too lazy to chase birds. He often turned up and leapt affectionately into her lap, where he would like purring and pondering his secrets. She took the tin of cat food and nodded. 'No problem.'

They talked briefly about the weather. Spring and early summer had been miraculously fine. 'We need some rain soon. It's so dry the soil's blowing away.'

That's right, Inge thought. I must do some watering. But, to her surprise, the next thing she said was, 'Do you believe in the one great love?'

'Goodness, no. All that's just hormones.'

'A biological drive, a trick to make sure the species goes on reproducing?'

'That's right. Still, I must admit it was lovely while it lasted.'

They shared a laugh. 'And afterwards?'

'Well, it's rumoured that some people live happily ever after, but I've never come across them. Have you?'

Inge had no answer. But when Kerstin had returned to her house and Inge was getting out the garden hose, she felt sure she knew some happy couples. She put down the hose, phoned Hilde and, without any preliminaries, asked how she and her husband had managed – they were happy together, weren't they?

Inge and Hilde were old friends, so Hilde just asked, 'What's all this about? Some kind of questionnaire?'

'No, no, I'm just thinking about love. It's Britta's fault, she's crazy about somebody and it worries me. She wants to get married.'

Silence at the other end of the line. Inge thought, She needs time to think.

'But, Inge, surely you remember the absolute hell Kalle and I gave each other for years? Dreadful quarrels. And, worst of all, the long silences. A lot of weeping and wailing – and too much drinking.'

'That's true.' But Inge remembered only dimly. 'How did you get through it?'

'Loosened our grip on each other. Gave way. And then things gradually improved.'

'Stopped projecting your own images?'

'That's a posh way of putting it but, well, yes, that's right. When I gave up my expectations of him, I could also allow myself to be me. If you see what I mean.'

Yes, Inge thought so.

She carried on watering the garden and came to the conclusion that she and Jan had never had a chance of success. That was that, and a shame, but wounds heal with time. Or do they?

That evening, Inge wrote in her diary: 'I have spent all of today trying to remember and analyse. Still I seem to have got no closer to understanding; I'm seeing things with the same old eyes and what I perceive are the same old images. I'm repeating old thoughts *ad nauseam.*'

Then it occurred to her that she had thought something new and that it had been important. She searched her memory and found the image of Matilde's beautiful face against the background of the London café bar: 'With him, I was no longer an outsider.'

Inge felt she had been an outsider from childhood. She had had no best friend and had belonged to no gang. The reasons were straightforward: she was a scrawny, awkward child, with no father and a mother who went out to clean. Then she grew too quickly, became taller than everybody else, a stick-like creature who lived for her schoolwork.

At seventeen her appearance changed and the ugly duckling turned into a swan, but it was too late. She never found a way to join in and believed she did not want to, that she despised those she saw as vain, giggling, flirtatious girls.

So, of course, when her prince came she fell for him at once.

She looked at this conclusion for a while, then drew a thick line through the whole sentence. It was not that simple.

CHAPTER 24

The plane took off from Stockholm Arlanda at seven
o'clock on Tuesday morning. They were served coffee.
Mira watched the stewardesses with baffled interest: hundreds of passengers, narrow aisles, occasional bumps – and
they never spilled a drop!

The coffee did not taste of much.

Mira was curious about everything. She's not yet realised.
Ingrid thought.

At Heathrow they had to wait an hour for the
connection to Edinburgh. On the plane they were seated
next to each other and José outlined the plans. He had hired
a car, which they would drive north from Edinburgh
airport. Apparently there would be a big bridge to cross and
then a motorway, the M90, which would take them to the
city of Perth. After Perth, they would drive further north-
west towards the Highlands.

'Remember, you'll have to drive on the left!'

José looked amazed. Then he smiled and said he'd better
rearrange his brain. Mira did not comment, but curiosity
shone in her eyes.

'The way I see it, we'll manage it in a couple of hours.
It's no more than a hundred kilometres or thereabouts,' José
said. Then he turned to Ingrid. 'Do you have your driving
licence with you?'

'Yes,' Ingrid said.

'Maybe you should sign the forms for renting the car.
Less hassle.'

José did not look at her but her anger was almost palpable.

'Come on, Ingrid, facts are facts.'

The man at passport control had caused José a bit of trouble. He had examined the Swedish passport suspiciously and said, 'So you're actually Swedish, Señor Narvaes?'

'Yes, I am.'

'Could you please tell me the reason for all these trips to eastern Europe?'

'I drive tourist buses for Swedish holiday companies.'

'I see.'

Ingrid was standing immediately behind him, red with anger and embarrassment. José seemed unmoved. Christ, he's used to this kind of thing, she thought.

They did not see much of Edinburgh: José did not take long to find the M90.

Driving on the left did not cause him any difficulty, but the sheep foiled him. They pottered along the roadsides, stopping as the fancy took them then walking on again, often just a few steps, their progress as slow as if they were sleepwalking. José had to wait for a long time outside a bright red telephone box. Sheep surrounded it and queued right across the road.

They could hear Mira laughing in the back seat.

They drove round the city of Perth, but saw nothing of it either. Then they turned off on to a smaller road, going north-west. It was twisting and narrow, patrolled by whole flocks of sheep, moving along in slow, solid waves.

Mira laughed again. José worried that they'd be late.

Later they were silenced by wonder at the defiant little road and its endless winding route past blue hills and green glens.

They passed villages and stared at the white, black-roofed

houses. Mira felt sure that Eloiza Drummond must live in a house like that. 'Somehow the name sounds familiar,' she said.

'Of course. Lots of people here have the same names. Hordes of McDonalds, for instance, and none of them has a thing to do with hamburgers,' Ingrid said. 'It's the names of the clans that have populated Scotland for thousands of years.' She giggled a little. 'There's a great tale about a Highland clan called Campbell. Since way back in history, they have been the bosses around here. One of them just couldn't keep his hands off the women and the story has it that he fathered 398 babies. That's the reason why there are millions of Campbells scattered all over the world now.'

José laughed, but Mira smiled rather tightly.

Then, suddenly, they reached a river and a little later a loch so beautiful it took their breath away. José stopped and they got out of the car to let the view soak into their souls, as Mira put it. It was called Loch Lomond and Mira asked if this was the lake where the famous monster lived.

'No,' Ingrid said, 'that's Loch Ness. But there's a song about Loch Lomond.'

She hummed it: '. . . But me and my true love will never meet again, on the bonny, bonny banks of Loch Lomond . . .' That was as far as she got, she could not remember any more words.

Only a short drive from there they saw the sign saying Crianlarich.

They had arrived.

José went into the pub to ask for the Drummonds' house, but came out again saying he couldn't understand a word they said. Still, they had drawn a simple map for him.

Just as they had thought, the house was white with a black

roof and sheltered among the blue hills. Eloiza was waiting for them on the steps. Her face was oval, thin and sharp-featured, her neck long, set off by black hair gathered into a low knot. Her mouth seemed sad, and her eyes cool but not unfriendly.

There are many women like her in Chile, Mira thought. Proud ones, who never give in.

Eloiza invited them into the sitting room, where a coal fire was glowing in the hearth. The room was worn, lived-in, heavy but cosy. The large pieces of furniture seemed the wrong size for the room, Ingrid thought. Mira almost disappeared into a huge leather armchair.

Eloiza served beer and lemonade. They spoke Spanish. Mira showed the photo of her mother and said, 'Everybody agreed they were very much alike.'

José had drawn a picture of his sister from memory. Without hesitation, Eloiza said, 'Yes, I recognise her. I thought so all the time, the name is unusual. We noticed her too because she was so young . . . only a child.'

All around the table fell silent. José translated for Ingrid in a low voice. Eloiza kept her eyes on Mira and said that the girl had been treated well in the camp. There had been no torture or anything like that.

The silence that followed was as heavy as the heat wafting out from the fireplace.

'She said very little. Sleeping at night was hard for her, so I often sat on the edge of her bunk and held her hand.'

Mira was crying now.

'We never understood what happened next, or why it happened. One morning Otilia ran out of the dormitory hut and straight at the fence. One of the guards shot her. In the head. She died at once.'

116

Mira, now very pale, searched for words and finally said, 'That's a comfort to know. That it happened so quickly, I mean.'

José went over to sit on the armrest of the big chair and put his arms round Mira. He was weeping.

Eloiza turned to Ingrid and said in English, 'I baked some scones this morning and prepared coffee. Come and give me a hand.'

They walked through the hall and into the kitchen. Eloiza shut the door, looked searchingly at Ingrid and said, 'Exactly how are you related to this family?'

'My mother is a close friend of Miras.'

'That's good enough. After all, someone should know.'

Ingrid's hand shook when she poured hot water on to the coffee grounds.

'Otilia had been made pregnant and gave birth to a child in that hell-hole. It was a difficult delivery, she was too small for the baby and tore badly down below. The child was taken away from her at once, nobody knew where to. She bled for days and was too weak even to whimper. She never cried. We could not reach her.'

Ingrid tried to steady herself by taking deep breaths. Eloiza went on, 'That's how things were before the morning when she ran towards the perimeter fence with some of their horrible dogs at her heels. The beasts were trained to jump and tear at the throats of people who tried to escape. I believe that guard shot her out of compassion.' She stopped, and set out the coffee things on a tray. Then she said, 'You must of course do what you think best, but I felt there was no need for the mother to know all this.'

Ingrid's voice faltered and she could hardly get the words out. 'You're right. Mira would be quite capable of going to

Chile at once to search for her grandchild. I'll tell my mother, but only her. And she knows how to keep silent.'

Ingrid's whole body was shaking as she helped to serve the warm scones with butter and ewes' milk cheese, then cake.

Nobody felt like eating, even though Mira said that they needed strength for the long journey home. When they had drunk the coffee, they rose to thank Eloiza and say goodbye. At that moment a large car pulled up in the yard outside. Eloiza stiffened as she told them her husband had come back earlier than planned. Two boys came dashing in through the door, shouting in incomprehensible Gaelic to the effect that they were hungry. A big man, a Scot in his late fifties, came in after them and stared at his guests without enthusiasm.

'We were just leaving,' Ingrid said.

At the sight of her his eyes grew brighter and he said, 'You must stay for a dram.'

But they said that, although it would have been nice, they had to catch a plane in Edinburgh.

Mira hugged Eloiza; Ingrid and José shook her hand. Afterwards, José tucked Mira into a makeshift bed in the back seat, using his bundled-up jacket as a pillow and Ingrid's coat as a blanket. She seemed to fall asleep soon after the start of their journey south.

The day was over, darkness fell. The two people in the front seats sat in silence; there was nothing to say. Behind them, Mira sobbed in her sleep.

Britta and Nano came to meet them at Heathrow airport. By now it was night-time, and pouring with rain. The great city was still glowing with light and the wet tarmac shone.

Mira phoned Inge from the hotel. They went to bed exhausted afterwards. Mira was weeping quietly. Britta tried

to whisper to her sister. For the first time in her life Ingrid
felt the loneliness of keeping a bitter secret.

CHAPTER 25

It was the Scandinavian summer of everyone's dreams.
Every day was bathed in intense sunshine and the evenings
were long and balmy. During the light nights of midsummer, rain cooled the air and moistened the ground.
Thousands of flowers drank it in and showed off with their
glowing colours.

Mira was recovering, but slowly. Melancholy clung to
her and she seldom laughed. Only her body was now the
same as before, energetic and eager. She was on holiday.

Ingrid worked as holiday replacement teacher at the
immigration learning-centre run by a neighbouring local
authority.

Inge was working on the proofs of her book and spent
her free time in her garden. The African lilies had come
into flower and she thought them impressive rather than
beautiful. But the nasturtiums were wonderful, their long
bright trailers cascading over the rocks, clambering up
fences and crawling across the patio.

One day Mira phoned and asked Inge if she would drive
her to the cemetery. 'Of course I will,' Inge said.

'You see, I have a family grave in Sweden. My mother is
buried here and somehow I've come to believe that the
dead children come to visit her.' Inge was speechless with
surprise. When Mira got no answer, she hesitated a little
then explained, 'I think I must have forgotten to tell you

that when Mother grew old I brought her to Sweden to live with us.'

Inge could think of nothing to say. Mira had cared for a mother who, by all accounts, had never cared for her. Inge remembered José saying, 'She was such a difficult person,' and Nesto, 'She was always mean to Mum, but I loved her all the same.'

Then Inge pulled herself together. 'I'll be with you in half an hour.'

That half-hour gave Inge time to recall much more. She remembered how once Mira's mother had withdrawn for a week, stayed in her bed and uttered not a single word. Her child had been left to starve.

This had happened after the father had left them. Hunger finally drove the little girl to the chemist to ask for help; she was given a meal by the woman pharmacist, who also found the child some easy jobs to do so that at least she had a little money of her own. But when Mira returned home, her mother took the money from her then got out of bed.

The idea of sending the eleven-year-old to school never occurred to anyone. She worked in a factory instead and for years supported her mother on her wages. Mira was not even allowed to keep enough for the bus fares to and from the great textile mill, which swallowed up hundreds of women into its great halls full of roaring machinery and whirling dust.

When she was seventeen, she married to get out of that inferno and ended up in another.

Inge remembered asking, 'How did your mother manage after your marriage?'

Mira had laughed and said that it had not been a

problem, her mother had started sewing trousers again. As always.

And Mira had brought that woman over here!

When they met in the street Mira sensed Inge's frame of mind. 'She was part of my fate. It's a daughter's duty to care for her mother.'

Inge did not understand and said nothing.

Mira's voice held a proud note as she said, 'Everything turned out well. I got her a small flat in a new block of sheltered housing. I just talked and talked until the officials in charge would rather have died than hear any more. They realised they'd never get rid of me unless they did what I wanted.'

She sighed and said, 'Money was a real problem, though, what with the plane tickets and the rent for the flat. The boys did what they could and helped me with the paperwork too. And she arrived. She hadn't changed a bit.'

Mira paused for a moment, then continued: 'I went to see her every day after work, looked after her and cooked for her. She never learnt much Swedish and never felt comfortable here. She used to moan at me about the cold.' She sighed again. 'Those years were hard work. And yet, you know, I grieved for her after her death.'

Inge parked near the church and together they walked slowly among the graves until they found the stone: Edermira Narvaes.

'Same as you?'

'Yes, I was named after her.'

On the grave stood a large pot containing a rose, covered in small red blooms.

'That's from Nesto, he comes here. He was the only one

who liked her. He always says that she was a completely honest person. I suppose that's true.'

Fair enough, Inge thought. Nothing to hide, only emptiness inside. But she did not say anything like that. Instead she said, 'I'll go and look at the church. You will want to be alone with the dead.'

Inge sat for a long time in a pew, searching unsuccessfully for understanding. When Mira came in, Inge told her that she admired her ability to forgive and asked if she had forgiven her father too.

'That was harder, but in the end I felt I could. I got a letter from a cousin who said that my father was seriously ill and could not afford to buy medicine. I started sending him money, about 150 kronor every month. That's a lot in Chile. Well, it was quite a lot for me too. Anyway, my cousin wrote to let me know that it was spent on morphine. That meant that at least I'd helped him to die less painfully.' She looked pleased.

'Would you mind coming with me to visit my father?' Inge asked, startled by her own courage. 'He's in long-stay care.'

'Yes, I will. But first you must tell me about your parents and their divorce and what life was like for you when you were little.'

Later, when they were sitting in Inge's bower, surrounded by thorny roses, Inge told the miserable story of her childhood.

For the first time, she thought.

She started to cry in the middle, but Mira did not let her get away with it. 'Carry on,' she said.

Afterwards they ate a simple supper and decided to go to Norrtälje the next day to visit Inge's father. 'I'll make us a packed lunch,' Mira said, which made the journey sound like a day out.

Now Mira has done to me what I did to her, Inge thought. She has asked me those deceptively straight-forward questions that force you to remember.

There he was. He seemed like a tree with a hollow trunk, lacking the vigour to reach towards the light and grow a canopy of leaves.

Inge wheeled him out on to the terrace. He said it was so nice of her to come. After all, it wasn't long since her last visit.

But it was, much too long.

'I've brought a friend. Would you like to say hallo to her?'

He looked at Mira for quite a while, then said, 'What a handsome lady. Something Spanish about her.'

'That's right!' answered Mira. She tapped her heels in a series of flamenco steps and snapped her fingers – it sounded as if she was playing the castanets.

Inge laughed but her father looked quite concerned and said, 'I didn't know you went about with classy people like this.'

Then he asked, as he always did, how her mother was. Inge answered, as always, that her mother had been dead for years. He sighed and said that it was good for her to have some rest. And, as always, the time crawled by.

On the way they had picked a bouquet of wild flowers, and Mira went to find a vase for them. Then he whispered, 'Where did you meet that woman?'

'At the garden centre.'

The answer was meaningless on its own, but there was

no point in going on. Words had to be exchanged, that was all.

Finally, the gong went for dinner. Inge wheeled her father into the dining room, they nodded at each other and said goodbye.

'Aren't you going to give him a hug?'

'No, it would just frighten him more.'

As they walked across the car park, Mira said, 'He is longing to die.'

'Yes, I think he's been waiting all his life for death.'

They stood at either side of the car, looking at each other, for a long time. Mira's eyes were bright and the whites looked startling against her brown skin. Her features seemed more finely cut than before, her expression more focused and her body slimmer. Daddy's right, Inge thought. Mira has gone through a lot but now she *is* handsome.

'You look tired,' Mira said. 'What are you thinking about?'

'About myself, about how poorly one knows oneself.'

Mira looked thoughtful. 'In the past I would have been so pleased if a man had called me handsome – even if he was old and bleary-eyed. It's different now . . .'

'How?'

'I suppose I must have become more like you. Who am I, really?'

'Don't, please, dear Mira.'

'What do you mean?'

'I don't know exactly.' That was not true. Inge did know. She wanted to hold on to the Mira who ate life with a big spoon and let everyone know how she felt about every single mouthful.

They opened the Thermos, poured the coffee and ate

their sandwiches sitting on a green bench, looking out over the long quay in the small town.

CHAPTER 26

Inge received a letter from Matilde. The Sweden–Chile Committee had invited her to give a lecture in Linköping: 'I thought we might meet there, but then I looked it up on the map. Your country is vast,' she wrote.

Inge phoned her. 'What are you going to lecture about?'

'I'm going to be very personal and talk about my love affair with Pedro Gonzales, then about torture, disappearances and death. Mira's daughter will be one of my stories, but of course without naming names.' She hesitated, then went on, 'I must speak about the resistance movement, as much as I dare. One section is called Pinochet's Long Arms.'

'Listen, I've got an idea,' Inge said. 'You will be here for the midsummer weekend, it's a big national holiday. Britta and Nano are coming and I'll bring them to Linköping so we can all hear you speak.'

'It alarms me in a way, but I understand.'

'You'd find it even scarier if you realised what it's like to celebrate the summer solstice in a lonely cottage surrounded by wild forest.' They both laughed.

Matilde asked, 'How do you mean? What kind of cottage?'

'Wait and see.'

Nano and Britta were arriving by boat at Gothenburg because Nano had wanted to bring his car, a Jaguar. It's a prop for his ego, Inge thought, then immediately agreed that one more car would be helpful.

She took pleasure in planning it all.

After the lecture, they would meet up at the old cottage by Lake Vättern that Inge had inherited from her grandmother. It was small and primitive, heated by tiled woodburning stoves and with an outside privy tucked away at the edge of the forest. But it was beautifully situated, with a view out over the long, turquoise lake.

When she told Ingrid her plans, the girl shook her head: 'Nano will not come to hear his mother's talk. And there's the weather – it's poured with rain every midsummer I can remember and we've been stuck inside the cottage playing cards.'

Inge looked searchingly at her daughter. This was not like her. Suddenly she was aware of something in Ingrid that had been there since her return from Scotland and that Inge had not wanted to see.

'Ingrid, what's wrong?'

'Everything. No – there's something I don't want to tell you about, it's so horrible, but I can't bear it on my own any more.'

And she told her mother what the Scotswoman had said to her. She stumbled through the story. 'Eloiza thought Mira did not need to know. Just that somebody close to her should have the facts. I promised her I wouldn't tell anyone except my mother. What are we to do?' She was crying now.

Inge seemed to have turned to stone, to white marble. Finally she spoke: 'We won't tell anyone. It would do Mira and her sons no good to know.'

The swifts, which had their nests under eaves, were swirling through the air over their heads. But for mother and daughter, looking at each other in mute despair, time seemed to stand still.

Then Inge said that, from now on, the responsibility was hers. 'Please, can't you forget now that you have shared the secret with me?'

'No, I've no intention of forgetting. I hate the upper classes in Chile and I won't stop hating them. Once I asked Matilde if she knew that her father had helped Pinochet with money and weapons. And she said yes, but that he was still her father and that she loved him.'

Inge told her about Mira and how she had used what little she'd saved to pay for her mother to come and live in Sweden. A mother who had never cared for her. 'Imagine, she lived here for years and her daughter looked after her all the time.'

'That's crazy,' Ingrid said.

Inge looked at the girl for long time. She remembered Jan. 'Maybe we Swedes are not very good at forgiving,' she said finally.

'But we are good at common sense. And that's got to be better than all these myths about blood and family and love.'

Inge did not dare disagree.

A couple of days later, Mira said, 'You know, Inge, there's something odd about you. You don't seem able to look me in the eyes.'

Inge stared fixedly at her and lied, 'I'm working on a devilish plan.'

They were sitting on Mira's balcony watching the darkening sky being sliced open by flashes of lightning. A thunderstorm at last. The next moment the doorbell rang. It was Nesto and José escaping from the rain and hoping for some coffee.

'This is perfect,' Inge said. 'I need you all to help with my plan.'

Once they had all settled with their coffee, she began, 'On the day before Midsummer's Eve, Matilde Larraino from the Chile Committee in London is coming to Linköping to give a lecture. Listen, and I'll tell you her story.'

She told them about London, meeting the Larraino family, Matilde's love for the young revolutionary and then about Nano and Britta. 'Those two will be turning up here tomorrow,' she said. 'I need you to help me persuade them to come to Linköping. After the lecture we'll all drive to my cottage and celebrate midsummer together.'

José and Nesto both looked doubtful, but José said that he'd seen the newspaper notice about the lecture, and that he had actually considered . . . 'But there's my family . . .'

'They're welcome too, of course.'

Nesto said, 'I do have problems with upper-class people from Chile.'

'So do I,' Ingrid said.

'They are human beings, after all,' Mira said, to their surprise.

Inge looked pleadingly at them all, her head tilted to one side. Nesto was counting carefully. 'We'll be nine people. How big is the cottage?'

'Tiny. And old and primitive. I'd thought we would hire some tents.'

By now they were all laughing at her eagerness. Mira said it sounded wonderful and José nodded in agreement.

Nesto joined in and said he knew somebody in an outdoor-equipment firm who would let them hire tents cheaply.

'Then there's the weather,' Inge said. 'This summer has

been so special but it stands to reason that it will be raining by midsummer.'

Ingrid came to her rescue: 'Four can sleep in the cottage and there's room for four more in the barn.'

'Just one left, then. And here I am, trained to sleep in tents at minus twenty-five degrees centigrade,' José said.

'The commando has spoken,' Nesto teased.

They agreed that Mira, Inge and Ingrid would drive on ahead and get the cottage ready. Mira took on the catering – oh, yes, there was a fridge and an electric oven.

Alone later that evening, Mira tormented herself with the memory of Inge's lies. All morning she had been unable to meet Mira's eyes, but when asked, all she could say was that she'd been hatching these midsummer ideas.

Lies, all lies, Mira thought.

It was almost unbearably hot in her kitchen so when she had done the dishes she went to sit and think on the balcony in the cool evening air.

Early in life she had realised that most people lied to her. It was shameful, especially since she'd had to admit that these cold fish, the Swedes, usually kept their word. Take the bureaucracy: slowly going through the motions, producing stacks of unreadable paper but, in the end, doing what it had said it would do.

She remembered how, soon after arriving, a social worker had tried to help her and her husband by providing family therapy and an interpreter. It was useless, her husband had never uttered a word. Finally, the social worker had arranged the divorce and a plane ticket for the husband, who wanted to get away from female-dominated Sweden.

She recalled that bank account. 'No, I'd never dare put

my savings into a bank,' she'd said, when the social worker suggested it.

Later she'd realised how silly this was. Certainly you could rely on the Swedes, but maybe not on individuals.

Except Inge. She had been truthful. But now she'd lied. Why?

Mira thought, I'll take her approach to things and just ask, straight out.

When Mira had her talk with God that night, a gentle voice suggested that Inge was hiding something to protect her. Mira was sitting in her bed, hands clasped, and whimpered a little. 'Why am I like this, so easily wounded?' she said aloud.

There was no need for Him to say anything, she knew the answer already: grief had broken down her defences.

'Do I have the courage to live, then?' she asked. God did not answer.

CHAPTER 27

Inge and her daughter also stayed awake late that evening. Inge did not mention what she had seen that afternoon on Mira's balcony: that there was an almost visible bond between Ingrid and José. The light between them was so strong they hardly dared look at each other.

Please, not this as well, Inge thought. But, then, they seem to be made for each other.

Ingrid was talking about Nesto, a charming guy but so

lonely. Somehow sadness was part of him and there was an appeal behind his kindness and generosity.

Inge, who had observed this too, said, 'What can it have been like for the children when all these unimaginable things happened and their lives crashed?'

Ingrid told her of José's helpless weeping after hearing the story of his sister from the woman in Scotland. 'There was something else in his face, though,' she said. 'Like . . . something had been confirmed, something he already knew.'

That rings true, Inge thought. Quiet, secretive José had the kind of lucid mind that does not allow memories to be stashed away in dark corners. Then she reached figuratively for the scalpel and said, 'But he has the best life now, a lovely family – his little boy is adorable and his wife is a lovely person.'

'Is she beautiful?'

Inge noticed her daughter's attempt to keep her voice steady. 'Perhaps not, but pretty. And, like most pretty Swedish girls who have the security of husband and child, she's put on a bit of weight and become rather bossy. I've only met her a couple of times, but she comes across as somebody straight, maybe naïve, but nice and a good mother.'

They stopped talking and listened to the owls hooting in the old oak across the road. Then Ingrid said she felt tired and was going to bed.

Inge walked upstairs heavily. She had done her cruel duty and felt unhappy about it. Tomorrow Britta's home and I ought to be delighted, she thought. But she was not, partly because she was also painfully aware that Mira knew she had been lying.

Not even God could tell them what they should do about this.

CHAPTER 28

The TV report said that the fine weather would hold over the midsummer weekend. Mira and Inge packed the car and just managed to save space for Lars-José and Kristina. She had taken a couple of days off and was coming along to help with getting the cottage ready.

Inge was thinking of Ingrid.

Ever since she had arrived back from England, a boy she knew from her old school had kept phoning and had even come to see her a few times. He had been looking intently at Ingrid's face, his pale blue eyes dark with longing. Now he had phoned again, the day Britta was coming home. He had rigged and launched his sailing-boat: would Ingrid like to join him for a trip to the islands over midsummer?

'Mummy has so much on her plate just now, I've got to ask her first.'

Inge said the trip was fine by her and that Ingrid needed to get away for a couple of days. She added that she liked what she'd seen of the boy, so Swedish and shy.

Mira had agreed that it was a great idea – from many points of view. She exchanged a long look with Inge. They both knew what had been happening that afternoon on the balcony.

When they packed the car, Inge felt a slight pang of compassion for the young sailor-boy, but dismissed it at once.

The two sisters met that evening when the Jaguar pulled up outside. Nano and Britta walked Ingrid to the jetty, where Åke was waiting in his boat. They both looked quite envious, but Ingrid said they had to go to Linköping and listen to Nano's mother.

'Those two don't find it easy to talk,' Inge said to Mira.

Mira had replied that only God knew how things would work out during the long solstice weekend. She seemed to change her mind when she saw the cottage and the lake in front of it. Here, surely, all would be well, she said, because this was God's own landscape, where the soul could find peace.

They never got round to discussing why Inge had lied.

Instead they aired and cleaned the old house, wrote long shopping lists and stocked up fridge and cellar. On the evening after the lecture, Mira wanted to serve a Chilean casserole, which would cook over an open fire among the rocks on the shore. Inge would buy the wine and food for a traditional meal on Midsummer Eve: cured herring, salmon with new potatoes and aquavit. And the first beautiful strawberries of the year.

Matilde was tired after the lecture, especially because the wait for the interpreter had made it much longer than planned. It was necessary, because so many Chilean immigrants had married Swedes.

The atmosphere had been heavy with pain and anger. Some people in the audience had wept in despair, but others had clearly wanted to resist the truth and to forget.

Inge was sitting next to Nano and glanced at him now and then. His face was a mask but he held Britta's hand in a firm grip. When Inge heard Britta sob and gave her a handkerchief, she noticed how the girl had to wrench her hand out of Nano's. His reaction was a wide, audible yawn. Inge suffered with him.

CHAPTER 29

At last they were all seated on the rocks on the shore of Lake Vättern. The fire was going well and Mira's casserole was giving off a powerful smell of herbs and spices. They were watching as the red disc of the sun sank slowly behind the dark hills on the other side of the lake, which was shimmering in the golden dusk.

'Will it ever become night?' Matilde whispered to Mira in Spanish.

'No. I can't explain properly, but the light has something to do with the North Pole. So has the dark. When the night starts it lasts for six months.'

'Honestly?' whispered Matilde, and Mira nodded.

'Yes, it's just awful,' she said. Then she thought she'd better be fair to her new country and added, 'The snow brightens things a bit, at least when it reflects the moonlight.'

Matilde tried to imagine this. 'What about the lake? Is it covered in snow too?'

'Well, no, but it ices over. You can walk across it to the other side. There's an old Swedish county over there, but I've forgotten its name.'

The young people went swimming. Diving from a tall rock, they shouted with pleasure and shock as they shot through the cold water. Britta flew into the glowing lake like an arrow, and Nesto and José came just after her.

Nano was left alone on the shore and his mind was frozen solid by one thought: they were bathing naked and his girlfriend was leaping about naked in the water with a couple of guys from a Santiago slum.

Matilde tried not to look at him. 'I want to go for a swim too,' she said to Inge.

'Right, we'll go into the next cove, behind the rock. I'll fetch soap and bathrobes.'

Mira said this was insanity, it was so horribly cold.

It was, but Matilde loved it and felt her worries loosen their grip on her body. When they stepped over the slippery pebbles on the shore to put on their robes, she said, 'This is like an exotic adventure.'

'Enjoy,' Inge said, and gave her a hug. 'Let's forget our grown-up children and all their dramatics.'

'But Nano is still stuck.'

'At least we've done our best.'

Mira called from the fire, 'Anyone who feels cold gets a shot of brandy. Come on!'

Matilde emptied her glass in one gulp and Mira thought, She's got what I have gnawing away inside her. Then she handed Nano a drink and said, 'Your mother is wonderful, you know.'

Then they all ate the Chilean casserole while the sun settled in the sky to the north-east.

Matilde had the cottage front room to herself. She fell asleep the moment her head hit the pillow. She woke early and heard Britta's voice, mumbling from her mother's bedroom.

Thank God, she understood not a word of what was said. She went straight back to sleep.

CHAPTER 30

The three women met over morning coffee in the kitchen. They were whispering so as not to disturb the young people. Somehow, they encountered language problems.

'This is ridiculous,' Mira said. 'I've spent fifteen years trying to learn a new language and suddenly it's all gone.'

'Speak Spanish,' Inge said. Mira's face lit up and, in her own language, she spoke of how much she admired Matilde.

Matilde hugged her with tears in her eyes.

Then they took their mugs and went to sit outside in the cool of the morning. Soon the rest of the house came to life. First came Lars-José. He tumbled out of the tent, struggling to get out of his sleeping-bag. 'Inge, help me. I want to go swimming.'

'I'll come with you.'

Matilde and Mira went on talking until Kristina turned up, her eyes still puffy with sleep. She called, 'Where's my boy?'

'Inge's taken him swimming.'

She calmed down and got herself some coffee. José crawled out of the tent, mute. Not a morning person, Matilde thought, with amusement.

But once he had poured his coffee, he turned to her and

said, 'I've had terrible dreams – because of your lecture, I think. You must understand that my own memories of the coup are chaotic. I was only eleven at the time.'

His eyes seemed to look into a long-lost past. 'I used to have one nightmare that kept recurring, about an old man who'd been hanged. Dangling from a tree. Even to this day I don't know why that particular image has stayed with me. So many other, often much more terrible, things happened. Like my brother being shot . . . and my sister . . . But tonight in the tent the old man was dangling from his tree again.'

Britta and Nano turned up next, got themselves coffee and made some sandwiches in the kitchen. The others needed only a glance at them to realise that they had not slept.

'It's so bloody light here,' Nano said.

José laughed and said, 'People travel from all over Europe to experience these light nights. Further north again the midnight sun shines all night long.'

'Ghastly,' Nano said.

'We'll get you some eye-patches,' Mira told him.

'No need for that. I'm driving to Gothenburg tonight. I'll take the boat back to England.'

They were speaking Spanish, but Britta had understood well enough. 'You do that,' she said, in English, and the silence that followed was so complete that the birdsong was almost deafening.

Inge returned, with Lars-José wrapped in a bath-towel. She put him on Kristina's lap and said that now she must rub him warm: 'I couldn't get him out of the water.'

'I don't have to do what Inge says 'cause she's so nice,' said the little boy. Inge laughed.

Nesto was the last to arrive at the coffee-table under the apple tree. He looked at Matilde, sat down beside her and put his arm round her shoulders. 'You're too beautiful and brave to be crying.'

Mira had slipped away to the kitchen and they could hear her light the old iron range for hot water to wash up. She was swearing at God and telling him that if he collected in a sack the tears wept by all the mothers in the world it would be so heavy that not even He could lift it. 'Do something,' she said.

But God did not answer.

Out under the apple tree, José rose, put his hand on Nano's shoulder and said, 'Come on, we're supposed to cut down a tree for the maypole.'

'There are lots of straight young ashes just behind the privy,' Inge said.

Soon they could hear the strokes of an axe and then the crash as the slender sapling fell to the ground. Nano was impressed: José had planned the cut neatly and calculated the fall to the last centimetre. They settled down at each end of the trunk to start peeling off bark and twigs.

'You handle a knife really well,' José said, and Nano smiled with childlike pleasure at the praise.

When they met at the middle of the trunk, José said, 'Look, why don't you just quietly get off to Chile and find your father's relatives – your grandparents and uncles, aunts and cousins? Get to know them. Listen to their stories of the guerrilla leader Pedro Gonzales.'

'What's the point?'

'It would help you come together as a person.'

'I would despise them.'

'Contempt is just a defence-mechanism.'

Nesto dug a large hole for the maypole in the middle of the yard. Then he ordered the women and children to go out and pick flowers. 'Off you go, into the meadows and woods and wherever,' he shouted.

Even Britta laughed. But Matilde looked worried. 'Is that allowed?'

Inge nodded calmly. They picked armfuls of purple vetch, golden buttercups and white daisies, a few corn-flowers and whole clouds of Queen Anne's lace.

Inge and Matilde walked along the soft path through the old pine forest. Matilde breathed in deeply and looked at the splendid trees: 'It's like being a church.'

'I agree, but I prefer this. No sermon to bother you.'

They roamed about for a couple of hours, mostly without speaking. They saw no one, except a small group of deer.

They only remembered the point of the walk on the way back and started collecting branches from the broad-leaved trees at the edge of the forest.

CHAPTER 31

Nano and Mira were kneeling side by side to tie the flowers and leaves on to the maypole. Kristina collected flowers into bunches and made wreaths. Nesto was looking around for a good crossbar. When he had found it, a debate started about the right height for it. The first decision was wrong – it was too high.

'It doesn't matter,' Inge said.

'Yes, it does,' shouted Lars-José, who was making a perfect nuisance of himself. But his father agreed, so they lowered the crossbar and could finally raise the maypole.

'Time for the toast to midsummer,' Kristina said, and went to get the glasses and a bottle of Östgöta Sädesbränn-vin.

'What, sweet little glasses,' Matilde exclaimed.

'You'll soon know why.' Mira laughed. 'The Red Indians would call this fire-water.'

Then Inge said, in Swedish, 'Let us raise our glasses and drink a toast to the longest day of the year,' which Mira translated.

Then they all shouted, '*Skål,*' and emptied their glasses. They breathed deeply afterwards and no one spoke for quite a while.

Inge and Kristina had set out the festive meal on a long trestle table next to the apple tree. The Chileans would not touch the cured herring, but everybody wanted the salmon. Nesto took two more glasses of aquavit.

Around midnight, they all went to sit by the fire on the beach. José played the guitar and Kristina sang some of the Swedish summer hymns: 'Wonderful is the Earth . . .' and 'The time of the flowers is coming . . .' Inge whispered translations to Matilde.

A little later, José was playing songs by Victor Jara. Mira and Matilde were singing, '*Yo no canto por cantar, ni por tener buena voz . . .*'

When the sun began to rise in the northern sky, Nano had fallen asleep in a corner by a rock. Nesto fetched a sleeping-bag and spread it over him.

CHAPTER 32

The next day over the morning coffee, Matilde tried to find words to sum up the experiences of the weekend. 'I'll remember every single moment,' she said.

'And so will I,' cried Nano, and poured out a shrill, exaggerated account of how ghastly he'd found it all, a deserted land with a sun that never set.

Of course there had to be an explosion – the tension had been enough to make the air vibrate, Inge thought. Then she was angry, and opened her mouth to tell him off.

But Nano would not stop. In Spanish, he started shouting at his mother. She was supposed to be a civilised human being, surely she, too, had hated this barbaric set-up. Like having to spend time with members of Santiago's underclass in this rotten old shed, which should have been kicked down a hundred years ago. Or using that rat-infested privy. Or watching men and women cavort naked in ice-cold water. 'Bloody barbaric country!' he shouted.

'It's my country,' Britta began.

She got no further, because Nesto stood up, stretched to his full height and deposited Nano on a branch in the apple tree. 'You forget you're speaking about my country,' he said.

'It's not your fucking country!'

'I'm a Swedish citizen. Do you want to see my passport? I've been to school here – got a good education. I've done my national service in the Swedish army. My friends are Swedish. And I'm proud of my country, very proud. *My country*, get it?' He drew breath then went on, 'I'd knock you senseless of your mother wasn't sitting here.'

'Nesto, please,' Inge said.

'Go on, Nesto,' Matilde said.

'I thought the upper classes were meant to have been taught good manners. Unlike us poor slum-rats. Seems I got it wrong. Your thank-you speech to Inge for her midsummer party was unforgettable.' Nesto's voice rose higher still with fury as he shouted, 'You're a useless little bastard, crap left over from the past.'

The loud voices had alerted José, who had been down at the beach with his family. Now he strolled across the meadow. He put his hand on his brother's shoulder and said he'd better calm down.

'You don't know what he's been saying.'

'True, but I can guess. This laddie is so scared he'd rabbit on about practically anything.' He turned to Nano: 'Get down, for fuck's sake.'

Inge turned to Britta and asked in Swedish, 'What are you thinking about?'

'Your father,' Britta replied. Then she turned to Nano and said, with deliberate calm, 'Go now. Just take your bloody car and go.'

'Alone?'

'Yes.'

When the large Jaguar had driven off, far too quickly, along the farm road leading to the motorway, Inge and her daughter went for a walk. They decided to look for the summer crop of chanterelles in the wood. They did not find any.

'It's too dry,' Inge said. Then they went to inspect the clearing with the wild raspberry canes, the sloping meadow next to the ruined cottage, where wild strawberries grew, and the rocky hill, covered in ferns, where they had once seen an elk. Britta had been little then. Then they visited the marshland where sedge and cotton-grass grew. As they turned back to the cottage, they were assailed by the smell of roasted lamb and realised they were hungry.

'I'll survive, Mother.'

'I know you will.'

'I'm so cross with Ingrid. She was right about him all the time.'

'It's so much easier to form an opinion if you're looking in from the outside.'

CHAPTER 33

Some strongly lit tableaux from the midsummer weekend would remain with them afterwards.

Matilde, who was crying under the apple tree, said, 'I've got to go back to London. It's such a shame, I'd looked forward to seeing Stockholm.'

Inge was just about to say that it might do Nano good to sort out the situation on his own, but Mira spoke first. She said in Spanish, 'Of course you must go and look after your boy.'

Britta tried to explain it to Matilde while she was packing. 'You see, if your values are fundamentally different there's just no way . . .'

'I understand. Still, Nano's problem is that he hasn't any values at all.'

'I know.' She hesitated and then she said, 'He blames

you, you know. Because you abandoned him. But I realise now that it isn't true.'

Matilde whispered a thank-you, but the chill between them was enough to make them both shiver.

Inge was busy on the phone, speaking to the railway ticket office and the local airport. Matilde could take the fast train to Gothenburg at six o'clock the next morning from Hallsberg. Inge would drive her to the station. The plane to Heathrow left at ten thirty and she would arrive by midday.

Then the last image: they were surrounding Matilde to say goodbye. The grass was dripping with morning dew. They hugged her, one by one, and told her they wanted to see her again soon.

Mira's farewell words were strange: 'No one can live on Earth without casting a shadow.'

CHAPTER 34

Halfway through July it started to rain, as everyone had thought it would.

The soil drank until it was thirsty no longer. One day it gave up. It could not soak up more water and soon Inge's lawn turned into a pond, the corn fields were rotting, the farmers were complaining and the nights were lengthening.

Ingrid's love affair – if that's what it had been – seemed to have been washed away by the rain. Perhaps the lack of good sailing weather had put paid to it. Britta did not hear from Nano. 'Just as well,' she said, though she was first at the letterbox in the road every morning.

Then one day José rang to speak to Inge. 'I've got a

strange letter from Nano. Could you come and have lunch with me in the bar next to the bus terminal?'

The low-pressure areas from the Atlantic passed over London too. Nano was pacing the floor of the large flat restlessly. 'I'm so ashamed,' he said to Matilde.

'You've every reason to be.'

They got no closer than that. Nano felt sure that she had not understood him, as usual. He wished he could scream, 'I'm in despair.'

He had never felt desperation before, only hatred. Hatred because all the bad things that had happened to him had been caused by his mother's desertion, and his grand-mother's – she had died when he needed her – and the raging old man. Frightened, yes, that was true, he had been frightened all the time – well, almost all the time. The beatings had scared him, but also the scorn and the demands, and the reproach in Matilde's eyes.

Britta had told him that he must stop seeing himself as a victim.

He tried writing her a letter: 'I knew from the start that you would not think my love for you good enough. I felt badly about that, but worse still was the terror when I thought you loved me. So I did what I had to do, I hurt and upset you. That gave you every reason to reject me.' He tore it to pieces and thought, I don't belong here or in Sweden or anywhere.

That was when he remembered what José had said when they were working on that tree. He had urged Nano to go to Chile and find his father's relatives. He had said, 'For as long as you know nothing about that part of you, you will be anxious and uncertain.'

Christ almighty, that bastard might have been right.

That evening he waited eagerly for Matilde's return. Hearing her key turn in the lock of the next-door flat, he felt frightened but pulled himself together and rang the bell.

'Please come in and sit down.'

But he did not sit down, just paced up and down, telling her what José had said. He detected a tremor on her voice when she asked, 'So are you thinking of following his advice?'

'Yes.'

'Fernando, I think it's a good idea. It could be a turning-point for you.'

'What about the old man?'

'We'll tell him you're going to inspect the old farm in the valley. It's his property.'

She had been right, as usual, he thought, when he saw the old man's face light up with joy at the travel plans. They sat talking for a long time after dinner and Nano was given a long list of tasks. He was to inspect the estate, contact the solicitor in San Felipe and check out any interested purchasers.

'It's all going to rack and ruin,' said the old man, red with fury at Allende, who had taken his farm into state ownership. Now, though, he had it back, and the land was still reasonably valuable.

When the old man had gone to bed, Nano returned to Matilde's flat. She was on the phone, speaking rapidly in Spanish, asking questions. His heart beat faster when he realised that she was talking to a member of the under-ground resistance movement in Santiago.

When she hung up, she told him he must get a new passport. He was to go to the London office and tell them that he had lost his old one. All the personal details must be correct, except that he should alter his first name to Fernie. Get handsome new British stamps on it, she said.

His grandfather would sign a document stating that he was travelling to inspect family property. The Chilean authorities would not object to that.

'They must have records on Pedro Gonzales.'

'There has never been any official mention of him being your father.'

'But the interrogations you underwent?'

'I should imagine all the records are destroyed by now. They can't be proud of what went on. Besides, money talks in Chile. It would surprise me very much if they caused any trouble for a member of the Larraino family.'

'How do I get into contact with ... my father's relatives?'

'Nano, listen carefully.'

She gave him instructions that sounded as though they came straight out of a thriller. He tried to think them ridiculous but felt frightened instead.

CHAPTER 35

Now that he was sitting in the plane, he was feeling as usual that everything had been arranged over his head. An idiotic idea, no doubt about it.

He was served breakfast, and cursed José Narvaes while he ate. That nobody, who spent his time chopping down trees, driving around in his stupid buses in that wilderness and handing out useless advice to complete strangers.

Then he went over his instructions again: he was to go

and find the large cathedral, then wait at the main door with Alcolea's book *La Catedral de Santiago* sticking out of his pocket. Just like some fucking spy story, he thought again.

But young people have an easy relationship with sleep. He dropped off and did not wake for most of the twenty-hour journey.

When he emerged into the elegant terminal building at the newly built Santiago airport, he felt full of expectation and almost happy. He was on his own, the master of his fate. But when he was waiting for his suitcase to come rolling along, he could hear Britta's voice saying, 'Now you've got nobody else to blame.'

Fear sent a chill through him. But there was something else still: that feeling of mastery.

The bustling crowds on the Plaza de Armas scared him, until he was drawn to one of the painters and stayed to watch the image grow in the large canvas.

The transvestites held no novelty value – he'd seen it all in London – so he made his way through the crowds and heard the young guitarists play and sing the songs of Victor Jaras. They reminded him uncomfortably of the mid-summer celebrations in Sweden.

He stopped to admire the arches over the doorway to the cathedral, the book clearly visible in his right-hand pocket. He realised that this was a land of suits, and that he was far too casually dressed in his jeans, grey anorak and white trainers.

The Catholic priest was younger than Nano had imagined him, but said, as arranged, 'I can see that you're interested in church architecture. Would you like a tour of the cathedral?'

'Yes, please.' At this point Nano switched off his ears, as he always did when being shown the sights. He thought nervously that the priest must soon get to the point.

'I would like you to pray with me.'

Nano followed him into one of the side chapels, knelt and listened intently to the prayer. In the middle of the Latin, the priest suddenly intoned that Gonzales was a common name in Chile, but that the origins of the revolutionary guerrilla leader Pedro had been traced to a village at the foot of the mountains. His relatives still lived there, he muttered, as he stood up and handed Nano a prayer-book.

'Read three Ave Marias to atone for your sins,' the priest said, and left. Nano remained kneeling, opened the book and found a set of directions and a simple map.

'Dear God, thank you,' he murmured, without really meaning it.

As he was leaving the cathedral, the priest was talking to new visitors, a group of German tourists who were concentrating on his description of the remarkable details of the great church. Nano put a banknote in the prayer-book and handed it respectfully to the priest.

Then he went to his hotel, asked for a good map of Santiago and its surroundings to the north-east, as far as the Andes. 'Can you arrange a car for me?'

'Of course.'

The man from the car-hire firm was also dressed in a suit, as elegant as if he had been on his way to afternoon tea. The car was a Volvo. Fuck that, Nano thought. 'It's the best car we've got,' the suit said. Nano showed his driving licence and signed the papers. When he drove into the dense traffic of the big city, he had to admit they made decent cars in the country without proper nights.

Britta's country.

Then he wondered if perhaps the car was a sign, but scorned the idea. He wasn't superstitious . . .

He drove through the endless suburbs and reached the valley he had to follow. The countryside was green, well-tended agricultural land. The engine of the powerful car was not strained as the road went steadily upwards, but Nano observed the Andes growing ever larger in front of him.

After two hours' driving, he reached the village. He went into the local bar for a beer and asked casually for the Gonzales family. The barman looked at him with a sly smile, winked and said, 'Just two more kilometres. It's a dirt road, but you've got a good car.'

Nano felt ill at ease as he walked back to the car. Why the fuck had the man winked? He looked at the houses, which seemed to spread up the slope towards the huge, snow-clad peaks.

Actually, no, not houses, sheds. There were some ancient caravans and quite a few decaying American cars of sixties' vintage, and hordes of underfed children buzzed round his car, calling to him and begging. The air stank of rubbish and latrines and something else, something he recognised but could not place.

He put his wallet and driving licence in the glove compartment, locked it and dropped the keys in his pocket. Then he got out of the car and walked towards the biggest of the sheds.

The door opened and a fifty-year-old man stopped in the doorway. Nano stopped too. They had never met before but immediately recognised each other. Nano's fear became surprise.

The older man was just as baffled, but controlled it more effectively. 'So,' he said, 'another of Pedro's bastards. Where do you come from?'

'London.'

'I see. Pedro laid another egg with one of the high-society sluts he conned out of their money. What are you after here?'

'I wanted to meet my father's family.'

'Is that so?' There was no doubting the warmth that seemed to flow between them. 'Well, now, I'm your uncle. Everybody in this family is crazy. The number-one lunatic was Pedro, the so-called revolutionary who had his war and his glorious death.'

'Is that the whole truth?'

'Whole what? Nothing in this world is whole. Or that's my opinion. What's your name?'

Nano hesitated, then gave his full name. There was a glimpse of interest in the man's eyes. 'That's right,' he said. 'I remember her well, Matilde Larraino, beautiful as an angel and a complete fool. She stole money from her father and gave it to Pedro to buy weapons. We smuggled the hardware across the mountains. So . . . she had a baby. We never knew.'

He was silent for a while, then said, 'The enormously wealthy Larraino family.' After another silence, he went on, 'You have a brother, you know. He's the son of the madam who ran all the whorehouses in Santiago. She's quite somebody now. Her son inherited them and developed the market rather well.'

'And what do you do?'

'None of your business,' the man said, and his voice

suddenly took on a threatening note. At that moment, Nano recognised the smell that hovered over this stinking neighbourhood.

'Beat it, now,' Gonzales said. 'Off you go to London, back to your pathetic mother. Give her my best wishes.'

Nano heard the threat in the man's voice, said goodbye and went back to his car.

He was so afraid he grated the gears. He drove off swiftly, downwards, always downwards. Just before joining the motorway to Santiago he was stopped by the police. They were polite, but an officer took him to the side and asked him for what reason he had been visiting Gonzales.

Nano's heart was pounding, but fear made him as cold as ice. 'None,' he said. 'I had decided to drive as far as possible towards the mountains. On the way I met some old guy in a shed by the road and spoke to him briefly.'

'What about?'

'The mountains. I wanted to know if there were some good climbing routes.'

'What did he tell you?'

'He laughed at me and told me that the Andes were no good for fucking tourists, which irritated me – I'm an experienced Alpine climber.

'Alpine?'

'Yes, the Alps, mountains in Europe.'

The police officer was still polite: 'Why did you ask for Gonzales in the village bar?'

'Someone had said he was knowledgeable about routes through the Andean peaks.'

'And what did Gonzales tell you?'

'He told me to bugger off.'

They searched the Volvo with the help of a dog. Nano had read about narcotics-trained dogs and realised what was going on. He showed his papers calmly to the officer, who kept coming back to his name, Larraino.

'Señor Larraino now, is he your father?'

'That's right. I'm here to inspect our family lands just outside San Felipe. It is all confirmed by my passport and other documents, which are in my hotel room in Santiago.'

The dog came back, tail between its legs. The police officer apologised. It was all over.

Never before had Nano felt so strong as when he steered the car through the Santiago traffic back to the hotel. He was dirty, tired and hungry, but inexplicably at peace.

When he had showered and was lying on his bed, a terrible anxiety struck him. What the hell was he supposed to tell Matilde?

It was a new kind of terror. He had been frightened before, but not by such things. What can I tell her? He was responsible for her.

Then it came clear to him. She must never know.

He was too tired to go and eat in the downstairs dining room, so he phoned room service. He stuffed himself with prawn sandwiches, washing them down with a bottle of wine. After that he slept through the noisy night in this city that never went to bed.

The next day he did what he was meant to do: drove the few miles to the family estate just north of San Felipe. The landscape was beautiful, green, gentle and well tended. He looked at the tall avocado trees, which stretched up twenty metres into the sky, and inhaled the lemony scent from the citrus groves. Maize and all kinds of vegetables grew in plots shaped like hillocks and surrounded by ditches filled with water trickling down from the Andes.

But when he reached the estate belonging to his family,

the picture changed with brutal suddenness: the land was neglected and overgrown with saplings. In the centre was the house, a sooty ruin. People seemed to live like rats in tumbledown houses made from mud bricks.

A hopeless place.

Back at the hotel he had phoned the Larrainos' family solicitor and arranged an appointment. Now he was installed in the man's office and said, 'Are there any potential purchasers?'

'Plenty,' said the solicitor, a pleasant-looking elderly man with kind eyes.

'Someone who could make a go of it?'

'Yes, indeed.'

The silence lasted for so long it became uncomfortable. Finally the solicitor asked, 'Are you telling me that the Larraino family does not intend to keep the property?'

'That's right.' Nano smiled with satisfaction. He had made a decision.

The solicitor, too, looked relieved. 'I'm pleased to hear this. You must understand that your grandfather was not . . . well, he was far from liked round here. He was autocratic, given to having his workers whipped. And he raped the women.'

'Oh, my God,' Nano said. The thoughts flew through his head. His heritage was terrible, both on his father's side and his mother's. No wonder . . .

Then he pulled himself together and said, 'Could you tell me something about the buyer you are prepared to recommend?'

'He's got a degree in agriculture but is not wealthy. You must accept a loan as part of the purchase price. But I'm quite sure he'll turn the place round and make it a working farm again.'

'Please send his details to me in London. Once I've seen the papers, we can conclude the deal.'

Before turning the car outside the solicitor's office, Nano stood looking at the Andes. They were magnificent, wild and flaming in the red sunset. He imagined the high winding passes and, along them, the family of smugglers called Gonzales traversing the mountains with their goods.

A startling thought struck him: this, too, was part of his inheritance. His father had been daring, an adventurer who risked death . . .

José and Inge were sitting in a suburban pizzeria, but neither of them ate much. Instead, José was slowly translating the packed pages of the longest letter Nano Larraino had ever written. They drank their coffee. José said, 'What the hell can I do? I say something that comes to mind, and he sets out as if he'd got an order. This is the result.'

'Has he been telling Matilde all this about Pedro's upper-class whores?'

'No. It seems he understands it would break her.'

'Maybe he does,' Inge said. Her words hung in the air, as she looked out through the window. It was raining. She was thinking about the boy who suddenly had a heavy secret to conceal.

'Maybe it isn't true. Myths always seem to collect round dead revolutionary leaders. You know, heroes have to be devils with women.'

'That's good. I'll say something like that when I write to Nano.'

'But not a word to Britta.'

'Of course not. But what can I do?'

'I've no idea.'

José returned to his minibus, dissatisfied. That afternoon he had an idea and phoned Inge before he left work. Would she please send a telegram to Nano in English to say, 'Please arrive Stockholm Arlanda on 3 September. I will meet the plane. We will travel to Dalarna County where I shall teach you how to paraglide. Please phone with arrival time at Arlanda. José.'

Inge dispatched it then phoned José. She said, 'I haven't got the faintest idea what this is about. Maybe I ought to tell you that you have no responsibility for what happened. But you're a strange man.'

CHAPTER 36

Mira braved the rain, she wanted to get down to the sea. It was grey and rough; restless, like her mind. She was remembering something Inge had said about a cat, the big tom-cat that belonged to her neighbours. It had been a passing remark.

'He's a big lazy thing. They get like that once they're castrated. Somehow they seem to lose the need for any excitement in life.'

They had gone on to talk about other things. Inge had not registered Mira's surprise. Mira had been staring at Inge and for the first time she had been struck by the similarity between her and the woman in Scotland. Inge Bertilsson, too, had a long neck, cool eyes and a face that would never give away a secret.

Cats, now. Mira had occasionally wondered about

Swedish cats. Why were they so fat and slow-moving? She used to think that they were a special strain. Now she knew: they operated on them to take away their lust for life.

As for herself, she hadn't had an operation but, then, she had never been one for sex anyway. 'You're like a meatloaf in bed,' her husband had said. Mira liked the description and tried her best to lie back and be a meatloaf with a hole in it. The result pleased her: four healthy children.

When she had just arrived in Sweden, the chattering about sex made her feel ill at ease. 'Sex' – the word alone was bad. The Swedes seemed obsessed with it. Both the men and the women! At first she found it repulsive, and felt ashamed on behalf of the naked girls on magazine covers and posters. After a few years the shame was replaced with a growing sense of having missed out.

Why had she? Well, her culture might explain it. Girls in Chile were never told anything except not to let men have their way. At first she had not understood the meaning of this.

Mira stopped and turned towards the sea so that she could feel the rain lash her face. An old agony gripped her. That new woman her father had abandoned her for, she was so ugly, so heavy. Mira searched for the right word and found it: vulgar.

Mira remembered the woman's mouth, which was so wide it seemed to run all the way across her lower face, ready to swallow anyone who came too close. She could picture her now, that lazy woman who always moved slowly.

So sensuously! She suddenly thought of something she had seen in a Swedish magazine: 'Nice girls go to heaven, but naughty girls go everywhere.'

Mother had been cold and beautiful, moved with precision and hated being touched. When Mira was little she had longed for cuddles and tried to touch her mother now and then. But she would be pushed away roughly, and the burning pain it caused was not just in the cheek smarting from the slap.

Now she could recall how the same thing had happened to her father: at his approach her mother would turn her back. That they had had a child together was a miracle, and that the child had grown and thrived had been thanks to her father.

Mira had followed her father about and he had responded with stories and songs, hugs and praise, outings and adventures. He had given her his own curiosity and insatiable appetite for life: see, watch, isn't it strange . . . ?

For many years now in Sweden she had tried to sharpen her image of her mother. There had been a rumour of another child, an older brother. Had it just been family gossip? Then she tried to imagine what had happened to her mother when she went to work with the cousins, farm-workers on a great estate to the south of Santiago. She had been thirteen then. '*O Dios*,' she said to the sea.

The same age as Otilia, when . . .

Her face was wet. Tears? No, just the rain.

Walking back, she was glad of the big mackintosh she had borrowed from Inge. It kept out the rain, though it was ugly, like most of Inge's things. Look at the sad grey house she'd turned into a nest for herself, crowded with dull furniture and all these books that sent up clouds of dust regardless of how often you cleaned up. Well, the mackintosh was functional, but it didn't rain every day, not even here.

The wind was behind her and blew away her irritation. She had been unkind.

Next, she started thinking about her marriage. She had been seventeen and he ten years older, left-wing and enlightened. He had given her a booklet with pictures of people having intercourse and babies growing inside her mothers' bellies and other useful information. But before she had finished leafing through it, her mother had taken it, torn it up and burnt it. Her face had been pale with fury and revulsion.

So the meatloaf woman carried on as best she could. Mira tried a little laugh, but it sounded more like a sob.

When her first child was on its way and she was growing bigger, her mother had called her disgusting. Mira had felt so ashamed she found it hard to leave the house to go shopping.

Her long strides carried her up the road to Inge's house. Inge took one look and said, 'Goodness, you are wet – come in, have a towel, I'll light a real fire and get the water going for tea.'

'Please, I'd like brandy in mine.'

'Of course, you mustn't catch a cold.'

By the time the hot drink was warming her, Mira could bury her embarrassment and ask, 'Do you think sex is the most important thing in life?'

For once Inge had no answers ready, just a few hesitant words: 'I shouldn't have thought so.'

'But remember what you said about the cat. You know, being castrated meant he'd lost the need for any excitement in life.'

Inge was baffled. 'But, Mira, don't compare us to cats. We don't run around back gardens calling out for sex.'

'You mean, we've got more interesting things to do?'

'Why, yes. Both you and I live without sex and still get a lot of enjoyment out of life.'

Mira smiled a little grimly and said that it was a shame never to have experienced it. It was like not having lived properly.

'But you've had babies, you must surely . . .'

Then Mira told her about her seaside walk, the thoughts and memories that had come to her. It took quite a while. After a brief silence when she had finished, Inge said, 'You've taught me something new.'

'What?'

'The problem is that we confuse sex and love.'

The silence lasted for some time, unusually so for Inge. Finally Mira asked, a little shyly, 'What are you thinking about?'

'I'm trying to find memories of happiness. Moments when I felt so truly happy that time seemed to stop. You know, your body and your mind are filled with light.'

Inge was gazing out through the window and her face glowed . . .

The children running ahead: Britta, who leapt rather than ran, and Ingrid, who held her hand and laughed. How old were they? Maybe nine and seven, the years when life seems to be all yours. The raspberry meadow on the slope down to the jetty, the children's mouths and cheeks raspberry red. Their light laughter mixing with the birdsong. A big beetle inside a tree stump. Ingrid wanted to know what it was called and loved the name. 'Maybug,' she sang delightedly. 'Maybug.'

'What kind of memories did you find?' Mira asked.

'Images of my children. My happiest moments were spent with them.'

Mira nodded and smiled. 'I have those memories too,' she said. After a pause, she added, 'But what did you mean when you said you still loved your husband, even though the possibility that he might turn up frightened you?'

'You snorted, remember? Quite right, of course. Because sex, in fact, was the only thing that formed a bond between us. At times I can still feel the lust he aroused in me. That's what I tried to say earlier – that women often confuse sex and love. At least the older ones. Young women seem more clear-headed.'

Her smile was a little ironic as she went on, 'People like me try to dress up sexual attraction as love, it looks nicer that way. There's something very . . . raw about the sex act. We often have a sense of shame about our bodies and desires. Many women find it hard to reach orgasm, and nowadays that is seen almost as crippling.'

They sat together in silence in front of the fire. Then Inge continued, 'I have sometimes wondered if there isn't a dark side to female sexuality. We take pleasure in submitting – which is nothing to be ashamed of, as long as love is the driving force.'

Mira was not sure she understood.

'That's why the young people are having such a good time. They're trying things out, playing with sexuality in a wonderfully shameless way,' Inge said.

'It's not always true. Look at Britta and Nano, in love but despairing.'

A shadow of anxiety passed over Inge's face and she answered, 'You're right. I suspect I've never really understood what people mean by passion. I'm just reviewing the arguments, as usual . . .'

'So you don't believe in fate?'

'No, I don't want to.'

'Listen . . .'

Mira told the story of Otilia, the girl who, even in the cradle, was so like her grandmother that people were amazed. The same dark, almond-shaped eyes, high forehead and finely drawn features. Her manner, too, was the same: she kept her distance and had a kind of dignity. And, like her grandmother, she had been raped when she was thirteen years old. 'She and Otilia,' Mira whispered. 'Mother had a child after the rape. At least Otilia did not have to endure that.'

Inge's heart missed a beat. She clenched her jaw. 'There's another big difference, Mira. Your mother survived and lived into her seventies. Otilia died at fourteen.'

'Of course that's true. But . . . it's also true that my mother wasn't really alive. She just survived.'

Inge nodded, but insisted, 'There were other differences. You've told me that Otilia was an affectionate child, that she'd sit in your lap and loved being cuddled. A sweet-natured happy little girl.'

'Yes, but maybe that was true of my mother too . . .'

Mira had noticed Inge's agony and decided to be brave. 'There's something you're hiding from me. You've known it for a long time.'

Inge drew a deep breath. 'Are you sure you want to be told?'

Mira thought for a long time. Then she said, 'No, I'm not. Let's wait. I'll tell you my decision when we meet again.'

CHAPTER 37

Summer returned as a heatwave by the middle of August. People were saying there was something odd about the weather, maybe to do with the hole in the ozone layer.

Inge's inner eye was focused on Britta, who seemed herself, smiling as always. But the corners of her mouth were tight.

Inge's publishers wanted her to write another book, but early one morning she decided to ask them for a break. She was too preoccupied just now. The theme they suggested was interesting, though: how to teach children to learn. Only a year or so ago she had known a lot about the subject. Now she felt uncertain ... about most things – yes, about everything.

She tried to get through to Britta. 'You know I'm always there to lend a listening ear.'

'Sure, but I've got nothing to say.'

'That all right, then.'

But it was not all right at all.

The tone in her diary entries became angrier, even furious at times. Why did *she* have to keep everyone's bloody secrets? Secrets that affected Mira and Nano, who was coming to Sweden to learn how to paraglide. And Matilde, who had been just an upper-class slut, used by Pedro Gonzales. She would not survive if ...

She wrote that she need not worry about Matilde, they were not having children together. She added an exclamation mark, then a large question mark, and wrote, 'But maybe that's precisely what we do have ...'

Then she started worrying about Britta again.

Ingrid had been offered a place at a teacher-training college. That was yet another story. She had wanted to train as a social worker and submitted her application to the college. Inge had not interfered, but had learnt enough about herself to dare to show that she had reservations.

She was sitting over her diary late one night, when Ingrid came padding into her room. 'Mummy, tell me what you have against me becoming a social worker.'

Inge closed the diary and leant back in her chair. 'There

are jobs and jobs. You'd be suited for some but not for others,' she said cautiously.

'What do you mean?'

'You would engage yourself personally in every case – the homeless alcoholic, the wife who allows herself to be knocked about, the children in need. There's actually very little you can do for such people within the social-service framework. I don't want to be sentimental, but I think you're too loving for a job like that.'

'But, Mummy, who's supposed to look after hopeless people?'

'People who can stay detached from them.'

'And I'm not one of them?'

'Look, Ingrid, I might be wrong, but what worries me is that it would . . . what's it called these days? . . . burn you out.'

A week later Ingrid came dancing down the path, waving a piece of paper. 'Mummy, I've got a teacher-training place! After out talk I applied and got a place because there'd been a cancellation.'

Inge's eyes filled with tears of relief. Ingrid was dancing around her now and noticed. She said, 'Dear Mummy, sometimes you're so silly.'

Britta travelled into the centre of town and met her teachers and classmates at the Karolinska Hospital medical school. The sisters managed to find a shared room in one of the student residencies at Roslagstull. Both were wound up: this was serious stuff.

During the week Inge would be alone again and felt that it was a good thing. Mira would drop in as usual, so companionship and talk would be on hand. There was something deep between Mira and herself. For the first time she thought of it as something more than just friendship. Something had been born the moment they first met in the garden centre. It had been almost like falling in love. It was not sexual attraction – neither she nor Mira could feel that way about a woman.

Inge sat with her diary for a long time. But she did not write down these feelings. Instead she wrote about the joy she found in their friendship, and how Mira had taught her to see with a newborn's eyes.

She wrote in big letters: 'NEWBORN EYES.'

Slowly she came to recognise that her previously intellectual approach to life had vanished. The walls she had built round her life had crumbled. It was not fate that had brought so many events of the kind that upset and hurt, the kind she could not cope with in her old common-sense way.

This had only happened once before in her life: when she got to know Jan, a man from another world. Meeting him had changed everything. Now a woman had done the same thing, someone who had literally stepped in from another world.

'I love her,' she wrote in her diary, then changed it to 'like her very much'.

José phoned and said he would like to come to see her. 'Are you on your own?'

Yes, I am. Do come.'

When he arrived, there were deep lines in his forehead. 'Don't you feel well?'

'No, I don't. Our secret about Nano arriving in September is uncomfortable. We're going behind Britta's back, you know.'

At once Inge recognised an element of her own anxiety about Britta.

'You're right,' she said. 'We must tell her, of course. How are you for time? I think Britta is arriving tonight on the nine o'clock bus. Ingrid is staying in town.'

Britta stepped into the kitchen with the bearing of a queen, tall and straight-backed, vigorously alive but looking more cynical than José remembered her. When she saw him, she smiled the old generous smile that spread all over her face. 'How lovely to see you.'

'I'm not sure you'd say that if you knew what I've got to tell you.'

He produced the long letter, seventeen sheets of airmail paper that fluttered in the wind from the open door. Inge lit a candle, which flickered in the draught. She shut the door.

José translated, searching slowly for the correct words in Swedish. Britta lowered her eyelids and her face looked as pale and cold as the August moon in the sky outside. She interrupted just once: 'What did you say to him?'

José told her and said he had never realised how important it might be: 'Learn to know both halves of yourself.'

'So he went there?'

'Yes, he did.'

'Alone?'

'Yes.'

The translation went on, so slowly that Britta had time to savour every word. The descriptions of the country, the encounter with the Andean smugglers at the foot of the mountains, the uncle who had recognised him as one of Pedro's bastards, and the police, who investigated his car with dogs trained to find drugs. Then the sale of the estate, the agonising about his mother and his decision not to tell her about Pedro.

She asked no more and made no comment. When José had put away the letter, he sighed and said, 'Now for the worst bit. You see, I felt responsible and, besides, I quite liked him.'

He held out the telegram with its jubilant message: 'Thanks a million. Arriving Arlanda 12 September at 12.30.'

In the silence they could hear the grandfather clock ticking in the study then striking eleven. Finally Britta said, 'What's paragliding?'

At last José looked happier. When he spoke, his eyes shone like an excited little boy's.

'It sounds really crazy,' Britta said. 'And dangerous. Do you think he'll dare?

'At the end of the course he'll be practising parachute jumping too.'

'Christ, no.'

'Why not?'

'He's terrified of heights.'

'Parachuting is the best way to get over it.'

Britta's eyes were round with surprise. In the end she said, 'Why am I in love with Nano and not you?'

'Such a shame,' José said, and they all laughed.

Britta took the letter. 'My Spanish isn't that great, but I'll get through it,' she said.

José left in better mood than he had arrived.

Britta went off to find a Spanish dictionary, said goodnight to Inge then turned on the stairs. 'Do you think Nano is going to grow up?'

'Let's wait and see.'

'You think there's a chance?'
'Britta, I haven't got a crystal ball.'

CHAPTER 38

'I've made up my mind. Tell me,' Mira said.

They had gone by car to the old forest to pick mushrooms and found chanterelles and a few large boletus. They were having a rest, sitting on tree-stumps and eating apples.

Inge sighed and, for a moment, the darkness in her eyes frightened Mira. 'She had a child,' Inge said plainly. 'Ingrid was told in Scotland. The woman there took her into the kitchen on her own. She wanted to let one of your friends know.'

Mira sat in silence, speechless.

Inge wept. 'No one knows what happened to the baby. They took it away.'

'Was it a boy or a girl?'

'No one knows that either.'

There was nothing more to say, not then. They threw their apple cores on to the ground under the birches and observed that the leaves were turning yellow. Another autumn was on its way.

Inge had parked on a twisting forest road. She realised now that she would have to reverse to get out. She was not keen on driving cars backwards. Having to peer through tears did not make it any easier.

They got out in the end and drew sighs of relief when the car turned into the road.

'Do you have any money?' Mira asked.

'Should have. My wallet's in the bag.'

'I want to borrow a couple of hundred to buy flowers for Mother's grave. Is that all right?'

'Sure. I'll stop at Läggesta.'

She bought a small rosebush in a pot. The flowers were sweetly, delicately pink.

In memory of Otilia, Inge thought.

'In a couple of weeks the frost will have killed them,' Mira said. 'Somehow that seems exactly right.'

They decided to prepare the mushrooms in Mira's flat.

'I'll make small beef meatballs. I've got the mince and the cream,' Mira said. Inge nodded. She wept until Mira told her to turn off the waterworks. There are times when crying doesn't help.

Later, when she was getting ready to go, Inge asked, 'Would you like Ingrid to come? She knows exactly what was said in that Scottish kitchen.'

'No, not now. Maybe later.'

When Inge hugged Mira she seemed smaller and stiffer: it reminded her of the spring.

Outside the evening was dark and cold. Relentless autumn was forcing itself into their lives.

Mira had a long talk with God. She started on the attack: 'How could you . . . ?

He did not answer and she realised the matter must be less rudely put: 'Please, God, don't abandon me now.'

She soon felt the gentle presence. He was with her.

'Thank you,' she said simply. 'Is the child alive?'

'No, it came to Me immediately.'

'Otilia, too, is she with you?'

169

There was a smile in the gentle warmth and the answer to her question was instant: 'Naturally.'

A little later in her conversation with God, Mira was made to recall the seven demons each person must encounter before they are allowed to meet their guardian angel. God said: 'Now you have little else to fear.'

'God, You must have forgotten what life on Earth is like. My home may catch fire, my sons may die in traffic accidents, I may get cancer or war break out . . .' She displayed all her fears to Him. 'I think little Lars-José is being bullied at school because of his beautiful eyes,' she said.

He did not answer. In the end she told Him the worst thing of all: 'The mad military could start a coup in Sweden.' But He laughed at that and she had to smile too. 'Well, you see, at times I can be really stupid.'

He agreed and told her to sleep now.

She obeyed and had a strange dream. She was in a bus and Javier sat next her, twelve years old and quite a young man. They were travelling north, towards the Peruvian border. She and the boy had been sent on a mission. It excited her. There were thick wads of notes in her bra, trade-union cash.

'You'll make it,' her husband had said. 'You look like a dull peasant woman so nobody will suspect you.'

At the border they met the soldiers and the customs men, weapons slapping against their thighs. She lied to them as she had been told to. She and her son were on their way to visit a cousin who lived in a village on the other side of the border.

In her dream she thought, So many Indians. Strange, she'd forgotten how many there were. The marketplace just across the border was full of wonderful things. There were nylon stockings, silk underwear, lots of jewellery and beautiful Indian textiles. People were laughing and shouting.

But she carried out her orders and went to see the man at

the stall at the far left-hand corner of the marketplace. She brought a couple of kilograms of gold rings.

Her heart was beating when she crept into the tent where people went to piss. She could smell the stench even in her dream. She managed to find room for the gold under her clothes.

Then they queued again to cross the border and the bored soldiers paid them no attention. Both she and the boy were dripping with sweat. *Dios*, the heat!

Her husband took the rings, sold them at a profit and gave all the money to the trade union. She was not allowed to keep a single ring.

In the morning she was sitting in her Swedish kitchen, reflecting that this was the first time her dream had been a real memory, image after image. Perhaps God wanted to comfort her.

Drinking her coffee, she returned to Otilia and one thought would not go away: it had been a girl, her little granddaughter.

She could cry over her. Then she showered, dressed and went to work.

Two days later she went to see Inge. 'The worst is over now,' she said.

She also told Inge about the dream. 'The odd thing was, it was true from beginning to end. As if we'd been filmed.'

Inge agreed that it was odd. Dreams were usually obscure and confusing, she said. One was meant to interpret the messages.

'It was good to recall, you know,' Mira said, and smiled. 'I really did smuggle gold across the border.'

Inge sat silently for a bit then repeated the words: 'Smuggle gold across the border.'

'What do you mean?'

'Maybe that was your mission when you came here. You brought us gold, close to your breasts.'

'Come on, Inge! Mira said.

But Inge could see how her words slowly took root. Maybe they would grow. 'I don't believe that your God sends you meaningless dreams,' she said.

'Let's go and check your garden,' Mira said. 'There must be things that need doing.'

Of course there were.

Lime the soil, though it was too early yet. First, rake up the leaves. 'One's never sure what's what in this damned country,' Mira said.

As so often in September, the sun shone and the air was like glass.

CHAPTER 39

Another postcard arrived from Colombo in Sri Lanka. 'All well. Regards, Jan.'

She put it in her pocket. She would never show it to anyone and never contact the police in England. Never again.

She was pleased, almost happy. He had survived and was getting on with life. She had been to Colombo once, had seen the narrow alleyways and the proud handsome Singhalese people. She remembered the two little boys who had been carrying a third, even smaller, with no legs, and the

172

police, who hit the begging children with their batons. On that journey she had learned something upsetting about herself. There was a limit to her caring and concern, and she had been miserly about her possessions, because the children stole like magpies. Travelling by bus on that miraculously beautiful island, she had been obsessed by a single thought: There must be air-conditioning in the next hotel.

What was Jan doing there?

Not even the girls should know, she decided, and hid the postcard in the secret compartment of her diary.

That evening Ingrid rang and said, 'Can you believe it? Marilyn got a postcard from Jan. He's in Sri Lanka and they told the police, who've started looking for him.'

Inge took some time to formulate an answer. 'Remarkable how keen the British seem to be, all this to chase one man. I suppose it's about the money.'

'Mummy, it's about more than that. Maybe I shouldn't tell you but he has been charged with rape of his secretary.'

'Oh, God,' Inge said, and her voice cracked. 'You must come here and tell me everything.'

'The truth is horrible.'

'I'll cope,' Inge said, and remembered Mira.

When they met for dinner that Saturday, Inge said, 'I've been regretting daily handing that first postcard over to the police in England. I've also wondered why you persuaded me. There's no law that demands the next-of-kin—'

'We realise that,' Britta said. 'But it hardly applies if the relative was subjecting you to. . .'

Inge was slow to understand. Then she cried, 'No!' She went so pale they were frightened.

'Mummy, listen. We were so scared, but he never got at

173

us. We've got Marilyn to thank for that. She never let us out of her sight for a minute and slept in our room every night. She drove us everywhere, including to and from the airport.'

Inge remembered the telegrams and the worrying. But the children had seemed untroubled when they arrived and she never looked for any explanations.

'Perhaps you can understand now why we were so insistent that the police should get hold of him. Mummy, Jan's dangerous.'

'And we detest him,' Britta said.

The silence grew, and became as long and cold as a winter's night.

'I thought I knew you so well,' Inge said. Again her voice cracked with fear. 'And I thought there were no secrets between us.'

'You're not as strong as you think, Mummy. And you're so unbearably good and so demanding – and so fragile at the same time. Don't you see that we didn't dare tell you in case you broke down?'

'Don't forget your insistence on being so bloody honest all the time,' Britta said. 'You're killing off real honesty that way.'

'I think I understand. I'm learning slowly.'

Inge got up and was surprised to find how shaky her legs were. She got Jan's postcard, handed it to Britta and said, 'Please see that it gets to the police in London.'

The rest of the evening they spoke little. Inge went to bed early, although she was convinced she would not sleep. But she could not get her mind round what had happened and instead her thoughts went to Matilde.

Poor soul.

Then she slept.

CHAPTER 40

'The one thing I've got in this life is money,' Nano said. He wanted to hire a car for the trip to Orsa. 'Why add to the wear and tear on your old Merc?'

'Up to you,' José said.

Nano rented a Volvo. 'I'm used to them from Santiago,' he said, and laughed.

'You can do this now,' the Englishman said.

'Only in my head.'

'Don't worry, once it's in your head, your body willl get on with it. You'll see.'

Nano ran up the hill, carrying the heavy wing on his back. He was running inside a black tunnel of fear and did not see the sun on the intense purple of the heather along the path. Mustn't show fear, mustn't, he thought, as his hands fumbled with the straps and he watched the six metre-wide delta-shaped wing spread out from the aluminium triangle in the centre.

Then they ran downhill for a bit, the Englishman next to him holding the line. He spotted the car, which looked the size of a beetle, far off down in the valley. Then came the tug on the line and the command: 'Jump.'

His heart was dancing a wild tango in his chest as he fell over the precipice towards his death. He thought of his mother.

Then he reached the up-draught and felt the blue air carry him. It held him and he was rising! Surprised, he gazed out over the forest, which looked like moss. Red doll's houses.

Far away, the airfield where he was going to practise parachute jumping later on.

Now there were only a few minutes to go before he must return to earth. He was amazed to discover that he did not want to and would have liked to carry on his birdlike flight for ever.

He obeyed his instructions and balanced his bodyweight forward. Elegantly he glided downwards, controlling his descent with the wing.

He landed. It was over.

The Englishman told José in Swedish that the young guy was doing well and would soon get the hang of it. Then he told Nano in English that he should get up a faster speed for the jump and that there had been a few problems with the thermals. They would train him in wind-awareness next morning.

Later, when he was alone with José, Nano cried. He wept quietly, but the tears poured down his cheeks. Oddly enough he did not feel ashamed.

José said, 'Let's go and get some grub.'

They fixed themselves a meal in the living quarters at Orsa. Nano was absurdly hungry.

After they had cleared away the dishes, José told Nano to do some homework. Nano lay down on his bed and found the chapter on up-draughts. The next moment he had fallen asleep. He dreamed about his delta-wing and saw to his surprise that it was yellow, the colour of the sun.

On the long way to Orsa they had plenty of time to talk. Dalarna County was beautiful at this time of year. Nano did not mention the golden autumnal landscape. It would have felt wrong after his outburst about barbaric Sweden. He thought he should apologise, but José was not interested in digging up old stuff.

He did not even ask about the Gonzales family.

José had sent a list of course literature about gliding and Nano had found everything he needed in London. Now he was given a tough test. José was impressed: '*Dios*, you've learnt a thing or two! I thought it was hard going, especially all that meteorology.'

'I've been taught how to study, I suppose, but this is the first time it's been of any use.'

They drove through glowing forests, past gleaming lakes, hill and valleys. Then at last Lake Siljan, a warm, shining blue spreading out in front of them, pretending it was summer still. They saw, one by one, the villages and towns along the shore: Leksand, Rättvik, Mora then Orsa, where their living quarters were.

'What kind of shoes have you got?' José asked.

'Only trainers.' Nano showed them and José shook his head.

'We'll go to Orsa and buy you boots with ankle-support and proper lacing. You'll need that for landing or you might sprain your ankle.'

Nano's belly contracted with fear. 'Are all the instructors Swedish?' he asked.

'That's why I picked this place: one of the teachers here in Orsa is English. I've talked to him and he's going to look after you.'

At three o'clock there was another lesson and this time Nano was not alone. Some of the others were computer geeks, some were students, so over-excited that a child could have worked out they were scared, and there was a photographer, who had planned to go gliding in the Andes to film the flight of the condors from above. 'Have you been to the Andes?' he asked Nano.

'Yes, just a month or so ago.'

'What do you think about my grand plan?'

'It's insane,' Nano said.

He flew again the next day, and the next and the next. Before every jump he was racked with terror. His heart was pounding and he was pouring with cold sweat. But every time the fear lost its grip and was replaced by a feeling of infinite freedom. There were glimpses, too, of an immense sense of peace, as if he was at one with heaven, he thought.

It stayed with him when he landed and he wondered if this was what people called God.

One night he took his courage in both hands and told José about his strange feelings. José was not surprised and said it was well known that gliders could go into a state of trance. That was why this school had decided that no flight would last longer than half an hour.

The night was getting cold and they were lying on their bunks in their sleeping-bags.

Half asleep, José said, 'Of course, I'm no psychologist, but I think these fantastic experiences have something to do with having conquered fear.'

On the Saturday, Nano did a parachute jump from an aeroplane. He thought it was easier than leaping off the precipice.

He got his certificate.

The weeks in the camp had passed quickly and the group parted with regret. They told each other than they would meet again next September when the air was clear and the up-draughts strong. But now – well, that's life.

The photographer said, 'I guess you're right about the condors.'

'How did Nano do?' Inge asked José, when they met at Mira's afterwards.
  'Very well.'
  'Was he thinking of contacting Britta?'
  'No idea.'
  'And how is Matilde?'
  'Listen, Nano and I didn't get personal.'

CHAPTER 41

Inge and Mira stopped meeting as often as they used to. Each sat at home and mourned, one over a violated child, the other over a life violated by a man she had loved.

Loneliness closed in around them like shrunken old garments, clothes that had been looked after but washed once too often.

Inge's straitjacket was fashioned, as usual, from guilt. She had known so much about abused children from her teaching years; they were evasive and hard to reach, locking away in their minds experiences too difficult and shameful to communicate.

And all those articles and discussions about incest. How could she possibly have thought that such terrible things happened only to other people?

She tried to tell herself that neither Britta nor Ingrid had shown any symptoms and that she could not recall any time when the old trust between them had ceased.

Not seen, not remembered . . .

Then, suddenly, a memory came to her. Marilyn had phoned and said they could not have the girls with them for Christmas as agreed. She had been as polite as ever but distant, too, which had meant that Inge asked no questions. She had just said, 'What a shame, they'll be so disappointed.'

'I don't think so.'

At this point there was a gap in the conversation, but Inge had not wanted to notice it. She was delighted to have the girls with her over Christmas.

She had a slight problem with the English wife as well. They had only met once briefly, in an airport. Inge had detested her, mostly because she was very good-looking but also because the girls had run to hug her.

That is how I was, how I am. This is what I did not want to see when I examined my face so intently in the mirror.

In the evenings she did just what Mira was doing: poured herself large whiskies and drank until her thoughts were clouded enough to set her mind free. She would wake in the small hours, haunted by questions. How far had he gone? How close had he come? The Englishwoman had watched over the children, but what could someone so small do against a strong man?

She suddenly remembered a comment from the London telephone calls: 'Mummy, he's an alcoholic.'

Inge was sitting bolt upright in her bed and created a sequence of scenes.

The small woman matching the big man drink by drink until she could bundle him into bed. And then going off to sleep in the girls' room.

What about the boys? Her sons.

Inge remembered how surprised she had been that the

children were sent off to stay in the country so often with their grandparents.

Christ, her life must have been so hard. I shall write to her.

Later that day Inge tried to compose the letter, but found herself unable to find the words.

She went for a long walk to tire herself so that she would sleep without the whisky. It worked, but in the small hours she woke again. It was four o'clock. Agony seemed to invade her body and she wanted to throw up, but could not.

That morning she phoned her daughters' room in the hall of residence to say she felt unwell and that they had to meet.

They turned up the same evening and said, clearly worried, 'Mummy, you've lost weight in just a week and you're as white as a ghost. What's wrong with your eyes?'

'Maybe they've finally seen something like the truth.'

Silence. It was a cold night and Inge could see the leaves falling from the trees on the common, the large ash tree first, as usual. 'Please. Tell me what happened.'

'We didn't understand much at first. He started to paw us, you know, put his hand between our legs and on our breasts and things. Then one night he came into our bedroom. He . . . had his cock out, and we were terrified and screamed. Marilyn rushed in at once. She pretended not to see but said quite calmly that if he'd come with her she'd pour him a drink. We stayed in bed, not speaking, we were scared silly. Later on we could hear him trying to climb the stairs and Marilyn saying that he'd better sleep on the sitting-room sofa. Next, she came to see us and said that we were to share Britta's bed and she was going to sleep in mine. I think that's when we got really frightened. He stumbled into his car in the morning and we had breakfast later on. Marilyn said she was really sorry, but we had to go back to Sweden. It took a couple of days to get the tickets and he wasn't home much but, oh, Jesus, we were so scared. She was watching us every minute of the day, so of course we realised things were bad. Two days later she drove us to Heathrow and we forgot about it on the way back. Well, we tried. Mummy, is that clear?'

'No, it isn't.'

'We honestly did not understand what had happened. Somehow it was disgusting and shameful. But whatever might have happened hadn't. Then there were discussions about us spending the Christmas vacation in England. That was really frightening. We were so relieved when you and Marilyn cancelled it. When it was time for the summer holidays, we told you that we never wanted to go and stay with Daddy in England. We thought you might object and start going on about the agreement that had to be kept. But you just looked so pleased – you beamed at us. And we stayed in the cottage for a whole wonderful summer – do you remember? We played cards a lot because it rained all the time. And told each other's fortunes with Tarot cards, do you remember that?'

Yes, she remembered. She had bought a book about Tarot in Linköping and placed the cards in the prescribed patterns. A cruel king on a black horse had turned up in the central place and frightened them.

Ingrid found it all horrible and Inge had said that they were cheating anyway, this was a whole body of knowledge and they were just reading bits from a handbook.

The rain had been beating against the roof and lashing the window-panes. The cottage had smelt of burning logs, warm blackcurrant drink and wet earth.

All three women spent some time remembering. Then Britta went on, 'When we finally realised what was going on, you know – all that discussion about incest – it seemed so awful to us we couldn't possibly tell you. And nothing had really happened, you must believe that. And, of course, we knew how much you still cared for Jan. And how foolishly loyal you were. There were times when we hated you for that.'

At that point Ingrid took over: 'There are reasons, naturally. Like, Marilyn is rather cold. It's possible that he wasn't happy at work, the English can be hostile to foreigners. And then he'd come home to his wife who wouldn't have any of it, at least not willingly.

'You said yourself once that all you had in common was sexual desire. And then he changed woman and it turns out this new one is a strictly brought-up English girl, who's not keen on trying anything. I think that's when he started drinking. Maybe he nicked the money as revenge for her rejection of him.'

'We only got round to understanding all this when we went back to London as grown-ups. We visited them only because we liked Marilyn, she was a bit like a big sister to us. Most of the time we were desperately sorry for her,' Britta said.

There were red patches on Inge's cheeks, but her voice was as cold as ice when she said, 'There are always a thousand reasons for evil acts. Not a single one can serve as an excuse.'

The girls exchanged a glance and smiled. 'Dear Mummy, when did you work that out?'

Inge smiled too, while she thought about it. 'Mira taught me.'

Afterwards they all tried to turn the evening into an ordinary one.

It was not a success. Inge was tired and went to bed early.

CHAPTER 42

The sun was shining and the darkness in Mira's mind seemed to lift. She said aloud to Otilia, 'Now you've got to leave me for a while, my darling. I must get out among people or I'll go mad.'

Then she did what she had done once before, made some dough and put it in a plastic bag. She took it with her when she set out for Inge's house. It's crazy, we haven't spoken for a week.

Everything was quiet. The house was sleeping. Mira tiptoed in at the kitchen door and put the dough to rise by the sink without making a sound. Did she dare make some coffee?

She crept out into the garden carrying her mug and drank it sitting in the sun. It was colder than she had thought and she decided to get back into the warmth. Back inside, the mug slipped out of her hand and banged into the sink.

Now I've woken them all.

Just then she heard bare feet on the staircase, light, soft steps. It's the angel, she thought.

But it wasn't the angel this time, it was the other one, tall and incisive. But she did just what the angel had done once. She walked straight up to Mira and hugged her.

'It's wonderful that you're here,' Britta said. 'Mummy is going out of her mind with sadness.'

Mira backed away a little and asked, upset, 'Why is Inge so sad?'

Britta said that her mother would tell Mira herself. Then she hesitated and added, 'But, then, maybe she won't.'

'Why not?'

'It's just possible that she'll feel too ashamed. Come on, let's bake the bread rolls, make the coffee and wake everybody.'

They set out a big Sunday breakfast and Britta lit a fire. Ingrid came running down the stairs, hugged Mira and said, 'What a racket!' Then she said, as her sister had, 'Oh, Mira, it's so wonderful that you're here.'

When Inge turned up, wearing her old dressing-gown, Mira felt quite scared: 'Look at you! What have you done to yourself?'

'It's such a complicated story. The long and the short of it is that I lost my self-confidence.' There was a pause and then she said; 'I'm not sure I can bear to tell you the whole story.'

Britta and Ingrid glanced at each other, but Mira became angry enough for the sparks to fly: 'You have spent months listening to me and my miseries. Don't think you can get away with this.'

Inge started uncertainly and brokenly. The breaks became so long that Mira groaned, and Inge turned to her daughters and said, 'Please, you carry on.'

'Well, at this point she had a postcard from Jan. We told her to send it to the police in England, but that made her cross and she started asking why we were out to get him.'

'And that meant we had to tell her . . .'

They told the story together, of Jan abusing his children and raping his London secretary, and how they had been saved by his English wife, while their mother had no idea what was going on.

'Even though there were signs,' Inge said.

'Didn't you talk to your mother?'

'No, we felt so badly about it. Besides, we didn't want to

cause Mummy more misery. But we refused to go to England for our summer holidays.'

'We were scared stiff of him.'

'I ought to have known,' Inge said.

'One of Inge's many principles is that one must respect other people's secrets,' Ingrid said.

'I can't say I've noticed that,' Mira answered.

Inge left the table to make more coffee. The others were silent.

Inge said, 'I was so certain that the three of us never hid things from each other.'

'Not likely,' Mira said. 'Everyone keeps secrets, which are meant only for themselves. Children are the worst – one's own, I mean. Never hope to understand your children.'

Britta and Ingrid risked a laugh. Inge asked earnestly, 'Why do you say that?'

'Well, mostly because one doesn't want to understand them. Mothers cling to their nice soothing pictures of the children. Happy Nesto, wise José, angelic Ingrid, clever Britta. It's so disturbing if the pictures change.'

Britta's teeth gleamed when she added, 'There's another angle. When the children grow older they'll defend their secrets to the last. If they didn't their mothers would eat them alive. I think kids who share everything with their mothers are really disturbing. They'll never be free of her.'

'I know all that,' Inge said. 'Theoretically.'

'I'm sure you also know that real confidences are rare and are shared only once in a while. These are special, beautiful moments, worth remembering for ever,' Ingrid said.

Mira thought of her encounter with Ingrid in the kitchen. Inge recalled meeting Mira in the garden centre. 'I know,' she said.

'You know so much,' Mira said, 'Maybe that's why you understand so little.'

'You're right. I often lose my bearings while I'm looking for explanations.'

'There are none to find, you know. Life can be cruel and unpredictable. No one knows who is going to get hit.'

'The science-trained part of me objects,' Britta said. 'Cause and effect happens, Mira.'

'Good for you.' Mira laughed. 'You stick to your guns, Britta. Just right for your age.'

'You sound like Mummy. Like the wise older woman doling out advice. Ghastly.'

'Very sorry.'

They giggled. Then they cleared the table and the girls got ready to leave.

'Did you see Nano when he was here doing gliding training with José?' asked Mira, when they got their coats.

'Yes, we went out for a meal in the Old Town.'

'How did it go?'

'Nothing has changed. It's a pity. Still, we seem to be . . . very close.'

'Britta, why didn't you tell me?' Inge asked.

'Mummy, you never asked.'

Inge drove them to the railway station so they could take the train to a station blessedly close to the university.

'How do you feel now, Mummy?'

'A lot better, I think. Please, would you tell me about Nano?'

'There's nothing except what I said, really. All the resistance I've been building up over months just vanished in a few seconds.'

'Did he seem changed?'

'Yes, thinner and somehow more assured. Tough at times. I didn't like it.'

They arrived at the station and said goodbye, see you soon.

But Inge stayed sitting in the car at the station for a long time. She was thinking about Britta's description of Nano and her comment, so apparently unreasonable, 'I didn't like it.'

Did strong men scare her?

'Dear God, help me,' she said aloud.

And what about angelic Ingrid, born sweet and kind? Was her kindness a defence mechanism, to make people lower their weapons?

No, stop . . . mustn't analyse. Ingrid was born kind and Britta was domineering as a baby.

But she was cold with fear when she finally started the car. The wind had got up and on the straight part of the road past the church at Angare the gusts were so strong that Inge had to hang on tightly to the steering-wheel.

Mira was still there and had lit the fire. 'I've been thinking about you,' she said.

'What did you think?'

'That it was not only your self-image as the good mother that cracked when you learnt the truth about the man you had loved for so many years.'

'True enough, I thought of that too. But I've had no time to deal with it yet.'

By now the wind was causing windows and doors to rattle and bang. It howled past the roof, subsided for a bit and left a scary silence before it hit again with renewed strength. The leaves were torn off the trees on the common in dense swathes, and large branches careered at furious speed through Inge's garden, ruining her borders.

'Dear Lord,' both of them said, though only one of them meant it. The phone rang, but it was only José. He told them not to go outside: the radio had been warning of gale-force winds along the east coast.

'This is no ordinary autumn storm,' he said. Then the line went dead and Inge could hear the telephone pole on the corner break like a matchstick and crash into the road. Mira tried to get a station on the radio, but it was silent. Suddenly, the electricity went and the house was in semi-darkness.

'Good that you've got a calor-gas cooker so that we can have a hot meal,' Mira said.

They lit candles and made tea. Inge thought it tasted of gas. They discussed what to do with the contents of the freezer if the electricity did not come back soon enough.

'This is almost like an earthquake,' Mira said.

Inge could see that she was afraid. Inge herself felt curiously excited, almost elated. Blow winds, blow it all away . . .

But she, too, was frightened when the big ash tree on the common fell with enough noise to wake the dead. The old giant's root system looked big enough to support a small house.

They decided to get some rest, found some blankets and curled up in the corners of the sitting-room sofa. Far away, through the roar of the wind, they could hear the sirens of ambulances and fire engines.

'God, can't you let it rest now?' asked Mira, but it seemed He could not hear her for the huge noise of the storm. 'Something odd is happening to me,' she said. 'Remember, I told you how I dreamt about the journey to Peru? Well, now I dream like that every night. Dreams that are reruns of memories.'

'How strange,' Inge said, and half sat up on the sofa with the blanket wrapped round her shoulders.

'It is. Some nights, they're bright early memories, but at other times they're as dark as hell, terrible. Like something to do with my husband, which I'll never tell you about. Then I wake from sheer despair, wanting to howl like the women in Graciela's house. Do you remember I told you about them?'

'Yes, I do.'

'I sometimes wonder if I'm going mad. But it doesn't feel as if I am. The dreams are more like . . . merciful gifts. I feel that God is nodding to me. Not comforting me, just nodding.'

'Does He think these dreams are good?'

'Yes, healing somehow. He wants me to see everything that happened as it really was.'

'Is that possible?'

'Yes, because you can't control dreams. You can't fix them.'

They had lit two candles on the table by the sofa. Mira looked at Inge in the flickering light. The lines on her face seemed more prominent and her eyes darker. She was looking back at Mira in speechless surprise. 'I do remember something I read once,' she said, after a while. 'I can't recall every word, but the idea was that God – or the part of you that is God – cannot reach you in any ordinary way. He has to use images that belonged to your own experience.'

By now Mira was sitting bolt upright in the sofa, so eager she ignored the cold. 'Please explain!'

'Well, I'm not sure, but the way I think it went was that because God is not a human being in our world, He cannot address us in words. He does not belong to our transient existence, which our words, of course, describe. When He wants to speak to you He has to borrow images and experiences from within your mind. Somehow there is no other way.'

'Please, you must be quiet now,' Mira said. 'I've got to think.'

But she did not think, just wrapped herself in the blanket and fell asleep. Inge stayed awake, listening to the storm and trying to understand how long the road ahead of her would be before she would see images of her life.

She, too, must have fallen asleep in the end. When they woke later that evening, the wind had died down.

Inge pressed the switch on the standard lamp and they both laughed with relief: the electricity was back. The radio worked and all the stations seemed to have news about the catastrophe that had hit east Svealand County. The roads were blocked by fallen trees and people were urged to stay at home.

They decided to ignore the advice, put on anoraks and boots and slipped out by the kitchen door. The destruction seemed enormous. Inge's garden had been massacred.

But the storm was over and the night was silent. They could see the stars. The new day would come with a clear sky and pure air.

CHAPTER 43

Mira had left for work wearing a pair of borrowed trousers. She did not own any, because she loathed what trousers did to women's behinds. But today they were necessary. She had to climb over fallen telephone poles and trees on the way.

The nursery turned out to be closed for the straight-forward reason that the roof had blown off. Parents and staff were standing in stricken groups round the red wooden house. The fathers were muttering about jerry-building and the senior teacher was already at the city council offices, trying to work out emergency solutions.

Mira went home and found that the panes round her balcony had shattered into a thousand fragments. The flower-pots had blown over. The balcony was strewn with African lilies and geraniums, mixed up with shards of glass and broken pots.

The rest of the flat seemed fine. She tried the telephone and it worked, so she called her sons and exchanged reassurances. She also tried to call Inge, but the line was dead.

Then she got on with clearing up the mess on the balcony.

Inge, wearing overalls and rubber boots, was wandering about in her garden.

The housing estate was crawling with electricians and there was an engineer up every intact telephone pole. Others were erecting new poles, lorries were rumbling through the streets and motor saws ripped the air apart with their whine.

Say what you like about Sweden, but it's jolly efficient, Inge thought.

For a long time she stood looking out over the common and remembering how pleased she had been to get the last house in the terrace, with its small site sloping gently down towards the parkland. It had been spared because of the old trees. The oak was still standing unbowed, but without a single leaf left on it. The sycamores were fine, probably all the better for having lost a lot of dead branches. The rocky outcrop, part hers and part the council's, had lost every ounce of soil from between its stones. It looked bare and impoverished without heather and speedwell. And what had happened to the crocuses, anemones and primulas?

Sod that, Inge thought. It'll be fun to start all over again.

Her telephone was still not working, but the hot water had come on. She showered thoroughly and with pleasure. Looking at herself in the mirror, she no longer asked herself what lay behind the image.

No more questions now. A terrible discovery and a raging storm had finished them off. She had learned something about time.

What?

Something that Mira had said that evening, when they sheltered on the sofa while the wind tore past the house.

The phone rang. So, it was working at last. She ran downstairs. It was Ingrid: 'Mummy, are you alive and unhurt?'

'I'm all right. My garden had disappeared, but I suppose it can be restored.'

'Four people died, you know. Three were in a sailing-boat.'

'They have only themselves to blame, really,' Inge said, hardheartedly.

'Maybe. Still, the fourth was a woman out driving alone. A broken tree fell on the car and crushed it. We were worried to death, until Britta got through to the police and learned that the dead woman was twenty-two and travelling back to her home in central Stockholm.'

'That's awful.'

'Did Mira stay over last night?'

'Yes, she slept here. She was really scared and kept rabbiting on about earthquakes. Actually, it almost looks as though we were hit by an earthquake round here.'

'How's the greenhouse?'

'Unharmed. Remember how you thought I was mad

spending all that money on armoured glass for it? I'm really pleased I did now.'

'Hey, you sound in a good mood.'

'It's odd, but I've always found catastrophes rather appealing. They heighten one's sense of being alive or something.'

Ingrid laughed.

The doorbell rang. 'Here are the men with the saws,' Inge said.

'We'll come round this afternoon. See you.'

There were four men, each equipped with a motor-saw, who set to work clearing the great fallen ash tree and the debris of broken branches and uprooted shrubs in the garden. Inge served them beer.

Mira phoned and told her about the balcony. 'That's the end of our African lilies,' she said. But she was upset when she spoke of the dead. And also about the nursery roof. 'Who would have thought things like that could happen in Sweden?'

Inge gingerly put in ear-plugs and sat down with her diary to try to remember what Mira had said that evening on the sofa.

'Everything changes when you see your life back to front. Nothing was as it was, I mean, as one thought it was.'

'Are you thinking of something in particular?'

'Yes, Otilia. But in the end it became impossible just to think about her, because what happened on that kitchen floor came back to life. She was not the only one who was raped.'

'You too?'

'Yes. It was horrible, but . . . in a way, I was used to it. The terrible thing was when my daughter fell silent and I thought she had died. And, perhaps even worse, the boys, glued to the kitchen wall with a machine-gun pointing at them. They just stared. Memories like these must be kept blurred somehow, you can understand that, can't you?'

'Yes, I can.'

'This week I've been wondering if the boys remember at all . . . But I'll never dare to ask them.'

Mira's accounts of her dreams followed, Inge wrote on, and every word said that evening fell into place. She underlined 'Nothing was as it was.' It sounded right – strangely enough, exactly right.

The phone kept interrupting her. Friends and neighbours rang to find out how she was. The woman from next door called and looked out over the garden, where the tree surgeons were sawing the old ash into sections. 'Fancy! You were so pleased about getting the site next to the common,' she said. Rather pointedly? Never mind, Inge thought.

Nesto phoned, at last, and said they would come round at the weekend and help her clear up.

Mira prepared for the clearing-up as if for a party. She came over on the Friday to check the contents of the freezer. Just as she had suspected, several of Inge's frozen fish-blocks had started to go soft during the power cut.

She got out all the fish to thaw and sent Inge to buy a kilogram of prawns and one of crayfish, two tins of mussels in garlic-flavoured oil, saffron and large quantities of dill. 'Believe me, I'll cook you an unforgettable fish soup,' she said.

Inge spoke to Nesto, who promised to hire a rotovator. She borrowed two large oil drums from a neighbour and phoned the council to let them know that she intended to have a bonfire over the weekend. In the circumstances, they could hardly refuse.

Then she drove into town to pick up her daughters.

Britta swore rather colourfully when she saw the garden. Ingrid wept. Nesto came over in the evening to inspect the scene and said, 'What you need is top-soil so I'll get hold of a lorry.'

'I hope you're insured?'

'I am, but I think this should be called an act of God.'

They went early to bed that night to build up their strength.

Inge shed not one tear, not even when the rotovator tore through her borders and fragmented the roots of peonies and delphiniums, clematis and roses. They dug up the remains of the thorny rose bower and she watched equably. It had been a mistake from the start.

Her little mountain was washed down by the time the lorry arrived with soil to pour into cracks and between stones. Mira was making stock from prawn shells and dill stalks and the smell came wafting out of the kitchen. The sun shone and took the edge off the chill wind.

The October day had about it something of the happy, determined 'Let's get on with it!'

They laid the table outside in the sun and drank a whole case of low-alcohol lager between them. The soup was divine, with added flavour from the smoke rising from the drums of burning leaves.

CHAPTER 44

The October Fest, as they came to call it, became a tradition in the two families. They got together for one October weekend every year and dug the border, raked up leaves, cut the lawn and ate a fantastic Sunday lunch.

Over the years there were more of them. Nesto married a Polish woman, as shy as a deer in the forest. Ingrid had two daughters before she was divorced.

Britta qualified as a doctor and worked in Africa most of the time. This year she had come home in time for the October Fest and took on the cooking of the meal, which, as always, was a magnificent fish soup.

Now she was doing the dishes in the kitchen. It was getting dark outside, but people were still raking leaves and the noisy old mower was going round and round the lawn.

When the last saucepan had been washed, Britta switched on the radio. What she heard made her freeze. A few seconds later she rushed out into the garden, shouting, 'Come! Come at once, all of you!'

It was hard to get through to Nesto and stop him mowing, but José turned off the engine and pulled his brother along. Soon they were all gathered in the kitchen and listened to the excited babble of voices from London.

For ever after, Inge would remember the scene, like a film still. Seven people, in various stages of kicking off their boots, rigid as statues in different poses. When they finally got moving again, the incredible truth had sunk in. Pinochet had been arrested in England, accused of genocide and crimes against humanity.

'Switch on the TV,' said Nesto.

Inge did, but there was no news. 'Wait,' she said, and managed to tune in to the BBC.

Ingrid and Britta took turns to translate into Swedish. The reporters were speaking against the background of library material: old pictures of Augustus Pinochet from his arrival in London for a back operation. Baltasar Garzón, the judge at the head of a Spanish Commission of Inquiry, had appealed to the British for the extradition of Pinochet to Spain to undergo trial.

The reporter said that Garzón's account of the charges made chilling reading. It was a study of cruelty and humiliation, based on thousands of testimonials that spoke of appalling experiences, but documented in a correct, legal manner.

Five thousand had been killed or had disappeared, and more than three hundred thousand had been imprisoned. Many of the prisoners were tortured. Almost a million Chileans had fled abroad.

The hardest hit were Chile's Indian population, the Mapucho people. Trade-union members had also been targeted, as were teachers, students and clergy who had aligned themselves with the forces fighting for democracy. In those groups, sexual humiliation was common. Two bishops, one Catholic and one Lutheran, had been called to an audience with Pinochet, who declared that the clergy was infested with Marxists. Consequently, they would be tortured to make them speak and killed to stop the infection.

The statements of both bishops were included in the Spanish charges.

In some reports, there was talk of the Villa Grimaldi in Santiago, which contained the most sophisticated equipment and the best-trained specialists in torture.

198

Inge's voice scarcely carried when she tried to say, 'That was the place Matilde said she'd been kept. They used dogs to rape her.'

Names were on the charge sheet: long lists of people who had been executed. Fifty-eight during the first days after the coup, then another sixty-eight a few days later. Then more.

The BBC continued to describe the murders of faithful Allende supporters, carried out by Pinochet's terrorists world-wide: a car bomb in the USA, a street killing in Argentina, an explosion in Rome.

The broadcast ended with an extensive account of a new law, introduced by Pinochet. Its provisions gave amnesty for all crimes against humanity.

He would be a free man in Chile.

When they switched off the TV, Ingrid caught sight of seventeen-year-old Lars-José. His eyes were black with fear.

'Let's have a cup of coffee,' she said.

'Mum might like one too,' he replied.

'Sure. Kristina, do you want to join us?'

When they were sitting at the kitchen table, Ingrid said, 'This is rather like a fairy-tale. The good people have defeated the dreadful dragon.'

Lars-José smiled nervously. 'So, you think this is a good thing?'

'I do, with all my heart.'

'I feel quite tired,' the boy said.

'We're tired too,' the little girls agreed. They were drinking fruit juice.

'Why don't you have a sleep upstairs? You too, Kristina.' Ingrid came along and tucked the children in.

'Maybe you'd better stay here,' Ingrid whispered to Lars-José, seeing that he was still very pale.

'Sure.'

Britta was in the kitchen, making coffee, piling on plates all the cakes in the house and opening a bottle of brandy. Inge and Mira were sitting close together on the sofa and Inge put her arm round Mira's shoulder, as she had once before. Like that time when she had felt she had done the wrong thing.

When they were ready to leave, Mira said, 'Nothing will come of it. The British will never extradite him.'

'Whatever happens, the arrest has great symbolic meaning,' Britta said.

Mira snorted loudly. There was no mistaking her view of symbols. Then, almost solemnly, she shook Inge's hand and thanked her for a wonderful day. 'I'll come round tomorrow, as usual.' she added.

Nesto said that, of course, they were not going to leave the garden in this state. 'Back to reality,' he said, making it sound like a proverb.

José went to collect his sleeping family. Walking downstairs, Kristina said, 'Ingrid really is an angel, you know.'

'It's true, so watch out,' he said.

'Why should I?'

'The thing is, they don't really belong on this ungodly Earth of ours.'

The Chileans said goodbye quietly. They seemed to be ashamed, and neither Inge nor her daugthers could think of a way to comfort them.

The silence hung heavily, both in the little terraced house and in the cars that rolled homewards through the darkness.